BORDERTOWN WHEELER

BORDERTOWN WHEELER

by

Link Hullar

Dales Large Print Books
Long Preston, North Yorkshire,
BD23 4ND, England.

British Library Cataloguing in Publication Data.

Hullar, Link
    Bordertown wheeler.

    A catalogue record of this book is
    available from the British Library

    ISBN   978-1-84262-774-7 pbk

First published in Great Britain in 1993 by Robert Hale Limited

Published in Large Print 2011 by arrangement with
Link Hullar, care of David Whitehead

Dales Large Print is an imprint of Library Magna Books Ltd.

Printed and bound in Great Britain by
T.J. (International) Ltd., Cornwall, PL28 8RW

For
Sharon and Lauren
(my best friends)
And for
Terry C Johnston
(who told me I could do it)

ONE

The young woman's sandals made scuffing noises as she quickly made her way through the dark, cluttered alleyway toward her home. She cast a hunted glance over her shoulder, eyes wide with fright, and stumbled in the night. Someone was following her. She could hear the voices mixed with the sounds of boots making steady time upon the hard-packed earth of the narrow pathway. Trouble pursued Juanita Alvarez this night. Trouble would not be denied.

'Madre de dios!' She whispered a prayer under her breath. Regaining her balance, the young woman quickened her pace as the voices and boots closed the gap that separated them from the girl. She was an attractive young Mexican woman of eighteen years. Small-framed and about five feet in height,

she could not have weighed more than one hundred pounds. Dark brown hair hung loose about her shoulders, framing a pleasant face with full lips and deep, soft brown eyes set above a small, delicate nose. Her dark complexion stood out in stark contrast to the white peasant blouse she wore tucked into a full, colourful skirt that swished about her ankles as she ran. Fear etched lines about her eyes. She gasped for breath as she continued onward through the darkness. Drunken laughter sounded from her pursuers. The voices and boots grew ever closer.

Turning a corner, the young woman risked another furtive look back. She choked back a cry of alarm as one strong brown hand closed upon her shoulder while another clamped tightly about her mouth.

'*Muchacha, silencio!*' A deep voice spoke in a soft, firm tone and the girl relaxed.

'Paco! *Tres hombres…*' her words tumbled out in a breathless whisper, '*muy mal…*'

'*Si, si, muchacha,*' the man called Paco interrupted. 'There are three very bad men behind you and they will be here soon. I understand little one. That is why you must hurry home. Leave the *bandidos* to Paco.'

'But…' the young woman's face contorted by fear as she began to protest.

'There is no time to argue, *muchacha*. You must go, now! *Rapidamente!*'

By now the men who pursued the girl had stepped into view in the confines of the narrow alley. Paco released his hold upon Juanita as he shoved her towards home. Without further delay he stepped around the corner to confront the three who now made their way through the alley.

'*Hombres!*' Paco's voice was deep, powerful, and challenging. 'I think you must have lost your way. The Americano bar is back on Main Street.'

The men came up short. Some ten feet separated them from the Mexican. They surveyed the man with careful consideration. Paco Montoya stood only five and a half feet tall. Patched cotton clothing and worn sandals made up his wardrobe while dark, black hair and a bushy mustache, flecked with grey, were all that could be seen of his features in the gloom of night. However, the baggy, threadbare clothing covered a well-muscled torso hardened by forty years of manual labour. While Paco carried no pistol, his large, calloused hands were tightly bunched into fists at his sides.

'Go back to your saloon, *hombres*.' Paco's tone grew cold. 'Your boss might own the town but he does not own the people.'

'Out of the way, Mex!' the man in the lead snarled. 'We're on the trail of somethin' good.'

The man who spoke was tall, a little over six feet, and probably carried two hundred pounds on his rangy frame. Light brown hair stuck out from underneath a wide-brimmed, charcoal Stetson while a middle-aged, battered face glared at the Mexican blocking his way. Stubble sketched his chin, and all three men smelled of cheap whiskey.

'Come on, Luke, let's take 'im. He ain't even got a gun,' one of the big man's companions spoke up with a nasal tone. He stood behind the tall man he had called Luke and close beside his other partner. Both men who brought up the rear were younger than Luke by a good ten years, but were already running to seed. While Luke was tall, fit, and healthy, his two friends were short, plump, and unkempt. Both men carried pistols strapped about their ample hips. 'We gotta catch up with that purty gal, Luke. We ain't got time to waste on this no 'count, Mex scum.'

'Go on home and mind your own business,' Luke spoke again as he advanced upon the stout Paco Montoya. 'Scat! Get on outta the way!'

Paco did not reply. There was no need to reply. He knew it was time to die.

Stepping forward to meet the challenge, Paco swung a hard right that connected with Luke's square jaw. The big man staggered back a few steps, stumbling into his companions who trailed close behind. Paco continued forward behind a left hook that brought fireworks to the head of the big man who fronted the trio.

'Why you mangy coyote!' Luke shook his head before charging forward to launch a looping right hand of his own. Paco ducked low and responded with a left fist that seemed to bury itself in Luke's hard belly. A right to the ribs brought a grunt of pain from the tall man while Paco allowed himself a momentary smile of satisfaction as he stepped back from his adversary. Luke struggled to regain his breath and his composure.

Too late, Paco heard the tall man's pudgy partners closing in upon him from both sides. Someone grabbed an arm from one side while another took a tight hold upon the other arm from the opposite direction. The two chubby cowboys snickered in the darkness as Paco struggled to pull loose from their painful grasp.

'Give it to 'im, Luke,' one of the men admonished.

Wiping a small worm of blood from his

lips with the back of his hand, Luke stepped forward to pound a combination of punches at Paco Montoya's head. A cut opened upon the Mexican's cheek, spilling crimson down his face. The tall man launched another torrent of punches that opened a gash over Paco's right eye as more scarlet streamed down the man's features. The blows continued as Luke unleashed a savage fury of revenge for the few blows he had sustained at the hands of the powerful Mexican peasant.

At last, Paco's body gave way under the cruel punishment he was forced to endure. His stout form began to slump in the hands of the men who held his arms, and they let him sag to the hard earth at their feet.

Luke stood back to observe the crumpled figure, while his two companions began to kick the man who now drew himself into a tight ball in order to protect his head and tender stomach. Laughing and shouting, the kicking continued until Paco lay still upon the earth before them. Luke looked on in silence as his partners gulped the cool night air. Mouths open, winded from their exertions, the two pudgy cowboys still exhibited drunken, crooked grins.

'You think he's dead, Luke?' one of the men asked.

'Hell, I don't know,' the tall man replied as he mopped the perspiration from his brow with a soiled bandana. 'Don't care one way or the other.'

'I care.' The man spoke in a menacing tone as he knelt beside the battered form of Paco Montoya. 'I want him dead.'

Suddenly, Paco held a knife that flashed silver as it cut a crimson streak across the kneeling man's biceps and chest.

'What the hell?' The man quickly pulled back and struggled to his feet as the shallow wound seeped scarlet into the fabric of his shirt.

Paco scrambled to his knees before attempting to regain his feet. He tightly clutched the bloody knife in his fist while his eyes screamed murder.

BOOM! BOOM!

A pistol sounded in the dark alley as two slugs from a Remington .44 caught Paco in the chest to slam him back to the earth.

BOOM! BOOM!

Another revolver exploded in the narrow passageway as the lead from a Colt .45 punched large holes in Paco's head. The Mexican's sandalled feet twitched for a moment before he died in a spreading pool of crimson.

'That's just one less fool peasant Mr Hollister has to worry about here in Grandview,' Luke dismissed the murder in a light-hearted tone as his two companions holstered their weapons. 'Come on, boys, let's go get us another drink over to the saloon.'

All three men headed back through the alley in the direction that they had come from earlier.

Crouched in the darkness, behind a pile of boxes and trash, Juanita Alvarez sat in terror and sorrow over the horrible spectacle she had witnessed. Sobbing silently in the night, she kept vigil over the bloody remains of the brave Paco Montoya.

'Big' Jake Hollister was huge. At six feet and six inches tall, the giant weighed in at over two hundred and seventy pounds of muscle and bone. The tailored brown suit could not hide the man's bulging biceps and broad shoulders. Hollister's brown hair had begun to thin and grey, while a roll of flesh had been forming about his middle. However, at forty-seven years of age, Big Jake Hollister remained a strong, powerful man.

Standing now in the middle of the wide, dusty Main Street of Grandview, Texas, with big fists planted upon his hips, Hollister made an impressive figure.

'Marshal Jenner!' Big Jake bellowed in a rumbling tone that roared and echoed through the late summer afternoon.

Jake Hollister removed his spotless brown derby and passed it over to one of his men who stood by his side.

'Come on out, Jenner! I ain't got all day.'

The giant stripped off his coat which was also received by hands eager to please. He began to roll up the sleeves of the crisp, white shirt while he waited. The big man's thin, grey-brown hair was plastered to his head with scented oil. His face was blocky and square-jawed, clean-shaven with a shapeless lump of a nose that sat under dark eyes sunk deep beneath bushy brows. The face broke into a leering grin that exposed yellowed teeth clamped tight upon a stubby, fat cigar. Hollister was happy. Massive, scarred hands made fists at his sides. He was going to beat a man to death.

'Come on out or I'm sending Morgan in to get you!' He issued a final warning after spitting the chewed cigar butt into the dirt at his feet.

'I'm comin', Mr Hollister, I'm comin'.' The voice squeaked in fear as a man finally stepped out of the law office that fronted the town's main street.

Marshal Toby Jenner blinked his eyes at the bright sun that hung in the clear sky directly over head. This south west Texas day was hot. Jenner stood just under six feet tall with a solid frame carrying some one hundred and eighty pounds. A checkered shirt was tucked into faded grey corduroys while a blue bandana was knotted about his throat. The marshal's features were rugged but not unhandsome with shaggy sandy hair sticking out from underneath a flat crowned black hat. His brown eyes screamed terror as they searched the grinning face of the big man who now stood in the street before him.

'What can I do for you, Mr Hollister?'

'You been holdin' out on me, Jenner. I don't like it!' Jake Hollister roared. 'Now, step out here into the street so's we can get down to business.'

'But, Mr Hollister, I...'

'I said for you to step on out here, Jenner,' Hollister's eyes radiated savage blood-lust. 'Unbuckle that gunbelt on your way, Marshal.'

Without another word, Marshal Toby

Jenner let his gunbelt drop to the street as he stepped forward to face Big Jake Hollister.

'You've been keepin' out an extra share of the local tax dollars for yourself, Jenner.' Hollister's voice relaxed now that his victim stood within easy reach. 'Your job was to collect the taxes from the good citizens of Grandview and pass the loot on to me but you've been gettin' greedy on me ain't you, Toby?'

The marshal let his eyes drop. He examined the toes of his scuffed boots, but knew better than to deny the charge levelled at him by the town's mayor and undisputed boss.

'My payroll wasn't good enough for you, so you helped yourself to my tax money.' Hollister's voice boomed once more so that all those assembled in the dusty street could hear the accusation. 'This town is mine, Jenner. The town, the money, the people…' he paused for a moment to suck in a breath, 'even you, Jenner. All mine!'

'Yes, sir, Mr Hollister.' Jenner raised his head for a moment as he spoke in a respectful tone, but was still unable to meet the dark eyes of the big man who now towered over him. 'I understand all that, but...'

'You're a cheat, Jenner.' Hollister closed the small space that separated the two men. 'And if there's anything I hate worse than a cheat, it's a cowardly cheat.'

Hollister's hard right fist exploded in Jenner's left ear. The man's scream of pain was interrupted by a powerful straight left that sent two front teeth down his open throat and smashed his lips to a bloody pulp. Raising his arms to protect himself from the blows to his head, Jenner exposed his stomach and ribs to a terrible assault from the big fists of Jake Hollister. Folding at the waist, arms now clutched about his middle, the town's marshal caught additional punches to the face and head before dropping to his knees in agony and defeat.

'Come on, Jenner.' Hollister had hardly broken a good sweat from his exertions.

'Least you can do is try to defend yourself.' The giant stood glaring down at the bloody figure who knelt before him. 'Get up and fight!'

Head bowed, Jenner let the Remington Over-and-Under .41 derringer slip from the sleeve of his shirt into his right palm. In one desperate motion, he raised his head and hand in an effort to blow a hole through the leering face that hovered above him.

Instead, before he could pull the trigger of the deadly little pistol, a huge hand closed over his and ripped the gun from his grasp.

'Just what I would expect from you, Jenner,' Jake Hollister roared an obscene laugh as he laid the marshal out upon his back with a vicious back-handed slap. 'A cowardly cheat is just the type to try a sneak gun in a fair fist fight.'

Jenner struggled to his feet looking about for a means of escape, but Hollister's men had ringed the two combatants. The marshal searched the hard faces that surrounded him in hopes of locating a friend. There were no friends. There was no place to run.

The marshal saw the giant lumbering forward and launched an attack of his own at last. Hard lefts and rights pounded the big man's soft mid-section, but seemingly had no impact upon the towering behemoth. Up through the centre came a powerful upper-cut that snapped Jenner's head back. A clubbing left knocked the marshal to his knees once more, while a looping right smashed him to the earth. Dazed, Jenner tried to roll but was brought up short by a crushing boot to his temple. Kicking, stomping boots, rained blows upon his body and head until Jenner felt consciousness begin to fade.

'It must be over.' Jenner's foggy brain fought to keep him awake. Through bloody swollen eyes he watched as Big Jake Hollister knelt beside him. 'Yes, yes, it must be over.' The marshal breathed a relieved sigh through a nose smashed flat across his face.

'Nobody cheats Jake Hollister,' the man

spoke softly now with his face close to the bloody battered features of Toby Jenner, 'and lives.'

Hollister's big hands grabbed handfuls of Jenner's sandy hair to lift the head a foot from the ground before smashing it back to the earth with a sickening thud. He repeated the act again and again until there could be no doubt that the marshal was dead.

Big Jake Hollister ripped the badge from the lawman's shirt before rising to his feet. His dark eyes surveyed the ring of men who surrounded the lifeless form of the man who dared to cheat the boss of Grandview. He searched the faces until he found the thin, pale features and grey eyes of Morgan Erskin.

'Looks like we need a new marshal, Morgan.' The big man tossed the star to the small, fragile man. 'You're elected.'

Morgan pinned the star to his lapel while offering up a slight grin for his employer. The little man stood only a few inches over five feet and could weigh no more than one hundred and ten pounds. A well-tailored grey suit covered his slight frame, while a matching grey derby sat upon his close cropped blond hair. His thin face possessed a sharp, hawk nose which sat below pale, grey eyes the colour of his clothing. High cheekbones and sunken eyes completed his predator's visage. The man's complexion seemed to match his eyes and clothing; shallow and grey in appearance.

He looked like a predator. He was a predator. Morgan Erskin loved to kill and he was good at it. The two Smith and Wesson American .44 pistols strapped about his hips were the only things beautiful about the man. With ivory grips and engraved silver plating, the two revolvers were a striking contrast to the man who carried them low upon his thighs. Morgan liked to use the guns. He used them well and often. Some people might point out that Jake Hollister never carried a gun, but they were wrong. Morgan Erskin was his gun.

'Get some boys to clean up this mess,

Marshal,' Hollister spoke again. 'I'll see you over at the saloon for a drink a bit later this afternoon.'

The new marshal nodded as the giant pushed off though the ring of spectators after collecting his coat and hat. Morgan looked at the battered form that lay sprawled in the street, but felt no pity or compassion. Instead, he allowed a grin to momentarily animate his features. Things were really looking up for Morgan Erskin. He had finally hitched his wagon to a real rising star.

TWO

'Thunderation!' The old man growled as he stepped lightly from the shadows of the barn's interior into the slowly setting sun of early fall in south east Texas. 'I'm hungry enough to eat a coyote,' he winked at the young man who kept pace with him while crossing the ranch yard to the iron water pump that stood before the house, 'probably smell like one too.' The two chuckled softly. Both were tired from a hard day of ranch work.

Isaiah 'Bullwhip' Wallace, now aged seventy, had settled the Bar W ranch in early 1851. His Texas spread had prospered over the years so that the small town of Wallaceville had been founded nearby. Bullwhip's lanky frame stood six feet in high-heeled western boots while the old man carried some one hundred and seventy-five pounds of rawhide tough muscle. A full, bushy, grey beard hung down to his chest with a small, turned-up nose poking out from the whiskers under flinty grey eyes. A wide-brimmed Mexican sombrero sat upon his head, protecting his bald scalp from the late afternoon Texas sun. Tufts of grey fuzz were clumped about the ears that stuck out beneath the big sombrero. Dressed in typical cowboy gear, Wallace never packed a pistol; instead, the old man carried his ever-present, coiled, seven-foot bullwhip in a strong right hand.

'Time to clean up for supper, son,' Bullwhip spoke to the younger man, his son-in-law, as he stripped off his soiled shirt in order to wash up at the water pump. 'Them gals is gonna have a good meal on the table soon now. We don't want to let it get cold on us.'

The old man's partner pumped the handle while Bullwhip splashed water upon his face and torso to rinse away some of the day's grime and perspiration. Old Wallace vigorously scrubbed with the refreshingly cool water before calling out for one of the towels that hung from a nearby wooden pole.

'Your turn, Wheeler,' Bullwhip called out as he stepped up to the pump handle himself.

The powerful young man pulled off the sweat-stained blue cotton work shirt to reveal a compact, muscular torso. Broad shoulders tapered to a flat belly and lean hips. Wheeler McKay was not a big man, standing a few inches under six feet, but his one hundred and sixty pound form was sturdy and well-muscled. A white, puckered scar on each side of his left shoulder was a lasting memento of two summers past when the man had faced down violent enemies of the Bar W. The enemies were now buried in the cemetery beyond the town limits of Wallaceville. Tossing his shirt into a pile with the older man's, Wheeler unknotted the bright red kerchief at his throat before removing the battered old Confederate cavalry hat with faded gold braid. While the hat was similar in appearance to the standard Stetson cowboy hat worn by many men in the old west, this hat had been a gift to his father from Confederate General 'Fightin' Joe Wheeler. Josiah McKay had honoured the general by passing along his name to his only son. Later, upon Josiah's death, he had passed along the hat as well.

'It'll be dark soon,' Wheeler commented idly as Bullwhip began to work the pump handle so that water spilled from the iron fixture. 'These fall days are gettin' shorter by the week.'

Wheeler bent at the waist to splash water upon his face. It was a handsome face, not pretty, with hazel eyes that showed character and strength. Brown hair, worn long, blew softly in the light fall breeze. As he finished rubbing wet hands over his form, Wheeler felt a towel thrust into his hands by his father-in-law. The two men turned toward the nearby house as the younger man dried off with the thick cotton square.

The house was a rustic structure of log and stone. The original one-room cabin now served as the centre for family gatherings, including meals served at the large pine table. Additions to the large living area included a kitchen behind the big room and a two-storey structure off to the side, made up of three bedrooms; one downstairs, for Bullwhip and his wife Rosa, and two upstairs, for Wheeler, his wife Laura, and their toddling daughter, Michelle. Clean shirts for both men hung just outside the front door.

Wheeler and Bullwhip were stuffing shirt tails into their jeans when each looked out across the range in the direction of an approaching rider.

'Looks like we got company, Bullwhip.'

'I'd say so, son.'

Both men waited patiently as a little pinto pony carried its rider into the yard at a steady trot. Upon the horse's back rode a small, slender Mexican man of advanced years. Thick white hair, combed straight back, framed an ageless face with deep brown eyes and a full mouth. The man was dressed in a loose-fitting white shirt tucked into sturdy black pants that were cuffed over black Texas cattleman's boots. He brought the pinto to a halt before the two men standing outside the front door of the Wallace home and called out a greeting.

'*Hola, amigos!*' The rider waved a hand in cheerful salute.

'Howdy, Carlos,' Bullwhip called out with a grin animating his wrinkled visage, 'get down off that critter and set a spell.'

'*Gracias,*' the man spoke again as he stepped down from the saddle with an ease that defied his advanced years.

'Won't old Ben be missing you here around dinner time?' Wheeler asked as he stepped forward to greet the newcomer with an outstretched hand. Carlos Mendoza had served as Ben Dalton's house servant for over twenty years. Now that the Circle D owner had reached his mid-seventies, he relied on the elderly Mexican more and more as both servant and oldest friend.

'*Si, si,* Wheeler,' Carlos flashed white teeth in a smile as he shook hands with the younger man, 'it will do him good to miss me at dinner time. He will appreciate me all the more when I return, no?'

'I expect he will at that,' Wheeler grinned in response.

'Care to stay for supper?' Bullwhip queried the guest.

'Of course, *mi amigo,*' Carlos chuckled lightly. 'It is no coincidence that I arrive here at the time my cousin, Rosa, should be putting one of her fine dinners upon that big table inside.'

'Let's take care of that horse then and get on with the eatin'!' The old man reached out a leathery hand to grasp the horse's reins and the three men headed off toward the large corral near the barn.

A few minutes later the pony ran loose in the corral as Carlos, Bullwhip and Wheeler approached the front door of the ranch house once again. Already, the sun had slipped just below the horizon and long shadows stretched across the yard. The Texas heat began to cool into a pleasant evening chill. Ten feet from the front door conversation was interrupted by a squeal of delight from a chubby little girl who toddled through the open doorway.

'Papa!' The small girl giggled as Wheeler lifted her from the hard-packed earth to hug the child to his chest in a warm embrace.

'Hello, girlie-girl!' The young man's face beamed with pride and happiness as the toddler snuggled under his chin. Wheeler kissed the top of her head before Bullwhip stuck out a finger to tickle under the girl's ribs.

'Can't your old grandpappy get any of them hugs you little critter?' Bullwhip held out his arms to take the girl from her father.

'She grows more beautiful each time I see her,' Carlos observed, 'just like her mother.'

'Flattery will get you everywhere, Carlos.' A soft voice entered the conversation as all eyes turned to the pretty young woman framed in the yellow light of the front doorway. 'Dinner's ready.' She smiled at her husband, Wheeler, who offered up a loving wink in return.

Laura Wallace McKay had recently turned twenty years old. Indeed, as Carlos had observed, she seemed to grow more beautiful with each passing year. Long, thick black hair hung past her shoulders framing a delicate face with deep green eyes. Her dark complexion and attractive figure were complemented by the simple print dress that she wore.

'Mother is waiting, gentlemen.' She turned to retreat into the log house. The men followed her inside, with Bullwhip carrying little Michelle in his arms.

The big common family area was as rustic and attractive as the home's exterior. The hardwood floor was covered by rag rugs in rich earth-tone colours. The furnishings were all handmade of local pine or oak. A big stone fireplace dominated the room while a large bookcase with glass doors stood to the right of this imposing stone structure. Leatherbound volumes filled the case; Shakespeare,

Cooper, Dickens, and others lined the many shelves from top to bottom. There remained a deep appreciation for good books in the Wallace and McKay family home.

Across the room Rosa Wallace was placing a large, steaming bowl of beef stew upon the plain pine table when she looked up to see her cousin, Carlos Mendoza, pass through the doorway.

'*Hola*, Carlos,' the woman flashed her relative a warm smile, '*bienvenido.*'

'*Hola*, Rosa,' the man replied, '*gracias.*'

The two had only discovered their family relationship in the past two years even though they had lived on neighbouring ranches for some twenty years. For much of that time the Bar W and Circle D ranches had been rivals with little relationship between the old neighbours. However, times had changed in these last two years, and, as the families became closer, Carlos and Rosa had managed to uncover a connection that made them distant cousins from the same old family line in Mexico.

'He already knows he's welcome, Rosa.' Bullwhip winked at Carlos, 'and he knows he's hungry too. Let's eat afore we all shrivel up and blow away.'

Rosa was a strong, stout woman of Mexican parents. In her mid-forties, her dark hair showed some grey and her face evidenced laugh wrinkles about her eyes. Even though a few extra pounds had begun to settle about her hips, Bullwhip Wallace's wife remained an attractive woman.

Conversation buzzed about the big table as the family and guest enjoyed a meal of tasty beef stew and hot biscuits. Finishing the last of the coffee, Bullwhip rose from his chair at the head of the table to address Wheeler and Carlos

'Would you gentlemen care to join me out front for an after-dinner drink?' The old man spoke with exaggerated courtesy accompanied by a gentle wink.

'Obliged, Mr Wallace,' Wheeler responded in keeping with the light-hearted mood.

'*Gracias,*' interjected the slender Mexican.

The ladies began to clear the table, with the assistance of the toddling Michelle, while the men crossed the big living room toward the front door. Bullwhip paused at the large bookcase long enough to collect three tumblers and a bottle of Early Times Kentucky Bourbon. They all passed into the cool night air before settling upon an assortment of three-legged pine stools in the yard before the house.

Bullwhip poured each man a generous shot of the fine Kentucky whiskey before passing each a long, black cigar to enjoy along with the drink. For several minutes, the men enjoyed the quiet of early evening as they puffed the strong cigars and sipped the smooth bourbon whiskey.

'What can we do for you, Carlos?' Bullwhip broke the silence at last. 'You ain't just here for Rosa's fine cookin'. We all know you wouldn't of left old Ben alone lessen you had somethin' important to talk about.'

'*Si, si,*' Carlos heaved a sigh as he shook his head in resignation. 'I have come to see the sheriff.'

Ever since Wheeler had found it necessary to kill the corrupt sheriff of Croly County in a violent range war, the young man had assumed the job on a part-time basis at the insistence of the Wallaceville community. While he had agreed to take on the job only as a temporary measure, over two years later he continued to serve as the county peace officer in Wallaceville and surrounding Croly County.

'What can I do for you, Carlos?' Wheeler's voice was gentle and sincere. He sensed that the elderly man was uncomfortable with this turn of the conversation.

'It is very bad, Wheeler, very bad indeed!' Carlos began, then hesitated before continuing. 'My grand niece, Juanita Alvarez, she is in much trouble. There is great danger for her.'

'I don't recollect that you have a niece around these parts, *amigo*.' Bullwhip scratched at his beard in a thoughtful fashion.

'No, Juanita lives south and west of here in the little bordertown of Grandview.' The old servant's eyes grew hard and his tone became harsh. 'It is the devil's own town, *mi amigos*. Someone must help the people of Grandview.'

'Tell me about it,' Wheeler prompted the old man to continue with his story.

'Our people there are held tightly in the grip of an animal named Big Jake Hollister. He came to the area three years ago after buying out a local rancher. Hollister has built his Box H into an empire along the Texas border.' Carlos caught his breath and brought his trembling voice under control. 'But Big Jake is not content to be a big *Americano* rancher. No, this tyrant must control all that he surveys. He owns the land and the buildings and now thinks that he owns the people as well. He has guns and men so that no one can stop him.'

'What about the law?' Bullwhip asked with concern.

'Jake Hollister is the law in Grandview!'

The old Mexican removed a letter from his shirt to hold out before him while he continued talking. 'This letter from my niece arrived at the Circle D this afternoon. She writes to tell me of her troubles and the oppression of our people in this hell-town on the border. She writes to see if her Uncle Carlos can help her.' His voice broke for a brief moment before he could regain his control. 'Wheeler, someone must do something to help!'

'Carlos,' Wheeler spoke in an even tone, 'I have no authority way down there. I'm only a county sheriff. Besides, this is state business. The Rangers ought to handle a situation like this.'

'Hollister is far too powerful and wealthy a man to be bothered by the *Americano* government,' Mendoza spat. 'His Box H ranch is enormous and the devil now serves as the town's mayor as well. Besides, your people rarely hear the cries for justice from simple Mexican peasants. There is no one to help them Wheeler. No one to help my Juanita.'

43

Carlos lifted his eyes to stare deep into those of the young peace officer's. 'No one but you!'

Wheeler returned the intense gaze of the old servant without flinching. He well knew the truth of what Carlos Mendoza told him. A small town tyrant with money, land, and political power could indeed come to dominate and oppress an isolated bordertown such as Grandview. Just as Carlos had indicated, few Texas officials would take seriously the complaints of Mexican peasants trapped in a situation of this type. Indeed, Juanita Alvarez and her people could be in serious danger. Wheeler's mind raced with these thoughts as his hazel eyes searched the old man's face, letting a minute slip by before he spoke in an even, quiet tone.

'I'll have a look around, Carlos. That's all I can promise you.'

'I never doubted that you would my young friend.'

By now, each man had drained the whiskey

in his glass. Bullwhip poured a second and final round of the Kentucky bourbon. Sipping at the amber liquid once more and puffing at the now stubby cigars, the men caught sight of a large form standing in the shadows nearby.'

'Evenin', Abe,' Bullwhip greeted the man who now stepped forward into the area lighted by the open front door and windows. 'You care to join us for a drink and a smoke?''

'No, sir, Mr Wallace,' the man spoke in a deep, bass voice. 'I just came over from the bunkhouse a few minutes ago.' He indicated the small wooden structure far across the yard that housed the Bar W ranch hands. 'I didn't want to interrupt while Mr Mendoza was talkin'.'

Abe was a giant black man. He stood some six feet and seven inches in height and could not weigh less than two hundred and sixty pounds. Dark brown eyes, a broad nose, and full lips set off the man's handsome features. His skin was deep brown in colour. Dressed in simple plaid shirt and jeans, the high-heeled western boots made him tower over the three men seated in the front yard. Abraham Lincoln Davis was a good hand. Even though he had worked for the Bar W only a few months, Bullwhip and Wheeler had come to value the abilities of the young man from Mississippi.

'Somethin' we can do for you, Abe?' Wheeler asked, looking up into the expressionless features.

'No, sir, Mr McKay,' Abe shook his head. 'I just came by to let you all know that we spotted a bunch of cattle over near the Circle D range late this afternoon. We plan to head out early in the mornin' to push them on toward home range. If you're lookin' for ranch hands we'll be movin' a small herd of walkin' beef steaks onto better pasture.'

'That's fine, Abe,' Bullwhip responded after taking another sip of the whiskey. 'Y'all do whatever you think is best. I ain't got no special plans for tomorrow anyhow. Anything else?'

The big man did not move or speak in

response to the old man's question. He seemed lost, deep in thought.

'Abe,' Bullwhip spoke again, 'I said, anything else?'

'No, sir.' The man shifted his eyes to Wheeler. He seemed about to engage the Croly County sheriff in conversation, but stopped short.

'You okay?' Wheeler asked with concern.

'Yes, sir,' Abe answered quickly, then turned to leave the small gathering of friends. 'Good night,' he called over his shoulder as he walked into the darkness.

'G'night!' the three men echoed.

Wheeler watched the man's broad back as he crossed the yard returning to the bunk-house. He wondered just what Abe Davis had upon his mind.

THREE

Shades of orange spilled across the south east Texas sky in anticipation of the rising sun. The pre-dawn chill found Wheeler leading his big black stallion across the ranch yard toward the big house of log and stone. The handsome charcoal was saddled, packed, and ready for the long ride to Grandview in the far south west portion of the Lone Star state. Horse and rider seemed eager for the trail.

'Hold on a minute, Jim.' Wheeler paused before the open front door. He had named the stallion after an ex-cavalry sergeant from up Nevada way. In fact, Jim had come out of the stock bred on the big man's horse ranch outside of Cornerstone in the Nevada Territory. The young man scratched between the horse's twitching ears while the animal nuzzled against his chest. 'I'll be right back,' he spoke softly as he turned to enter the house.

Passing through the front door, the young man smelled coffee. He gave a curious look toward the kitchen door in time to see Bull-whip push through the opening with two steaming mugs filled with hot, black coffee. Wheeler stepped off the width of the room to find a seat at the big pine table with the bewhiskered old man. For several minutes they sipped the strong, thick brew in silence.

'You don't have to go, you know?' Bull-whip focused those flinty grey eyes upon the face of his son-in-law. 'Ain't really none of your affair.'

'You'd go.' A faint smile played about the younger man's lips while animating his hazel eyes.

'I reckon I would at that,' the old man heaved a sigh before continuing, 'but I'd be damn careful about it. I've heard of this Hollister feller and his Box H ranch. Like

Carlos said, the law can't touch him. He's got all the land and power he needs to keep his little corner of Texas tight under his thumb. That Big Jake is a mean 'un, son, and you'd best make no mistake about it; Grandview is a nest of sidewinders that you're about to stir with a stick. Take care that you don't get bit.'

'I'll be careful, Bullwhip.' Wheeler drained the cup before replacing it on the table. 'I've got to go.'

'Watch yourself,' the old man gave his companion's shoulder an affectionate slap, 'and don't worry none about Laura and Michelle. Rosa and I will take good care of them.'

'Never thought any different,' Wheeler smiled. 'I'm off for Wallaceville to stock up on a few supplies, then I'll pick up the trail to Grandview from there. Y'all take care.'

'Same to you.' Bullwhip rose from his chair along with Wheeler. The Bar W rancher carried the empty mugs into the kitchen while his son-in-law crossed the big room to a set of pegs just inside the front door.

Wheeler was dressed in faded denims, cuffed at the ankle above cattleman's boots, and a plain blue work shirt open at the neck. Reaching the wooden pegs, he removed a bright red kerchief which he knotted about his throat. He then took down a plain, well-worn gunbelt which he strapped about his hips. Snug in the leather holster at his right hip sat a blue Colt .45 Peacemaker with smooth walnut grips. On his left rode a big Bowie blade in a decorative Indian sheath. Next, he pulled on a worn, stained old buckskin jacket trimmed in fringe and Indian bead designs. The old coat had been a gift from famed gunman Elijah West many years ago. It would serve to keep away the morning chill in the air on these fall days. Finally, he reached for the worn Confederate cavalry hat left to him by his father. Tugging the hat into place, he stepped through the front door to be greeted by a spirited nicker from Jim. The big charcoal was obviously ready to stretch his legs. Wheeler checked the Winchester .44-40 carefully resting in his saddle sheath, then put a foot in a stirrup to raise himself into the saddle.

'You were just going to ride off on that big horse without even saying goodbye?' A soft voice broke through the early morning quiet. He turned to find Laura standing barefoot in her long calico nightdress with small fists firmly planted upon her hips. Her tone was mockingly angry. 'I think the girl you leave behind at least deserves a kiss before you go.'

Wheeler smiled as he removed his boot from the stirrup to close the gap between them. Taking Laura in his arms the two hugged tightly in a warm embrace.

'I thought we agreed to say our goodbyes last night,' he spoke gently after he kissed the top of her head.

'You agreed,' she replied playfully, 'I just didn't argue with you.'

'You get more like your father every day...'

'Is that so!' Laura pretended to pout.

'But you're a lot prettier,' Wheeler chuckled as Laura kissed him on the cheek.

'That's better.' She smiled while resting her head upon his chest.

'I told Michelle goodbye when I tucked her in bed last night,' a father's love evident in the young man's voice, 'but tell her again and remind her that I'll be home as soon as I can.'

'I'll tell her, Wheeler.' She lifted her head. Their lips touched in a tender kiss. 'You be careful.'

'You goin' to Grandview or you gonna lollygag around here the whole dadblasted mornin'?' Bullwhip bellowed as he stepped through the doorway into the ranch yard. 'Thunderation, son, you've wasted half the day already!'

Wheeler winked at Laura as he stepped into the saddle. Bullwhip moved forward to put an arm around his daughter's shoulders. Without another word, the young man touched heels to the big stallion so that the charcoal streaked out of the ranch yard into the rising sun. The old man stood with the young woman watching horse and rider grow smaller before vanishing into the horizon.

Jim thundered across the range for several minutes before his master slowed him to a steady trot. They had some hard miles before them in the coming days. There was no need to use up the animal's energy and stamina with a prolonged gallop. A man travelling through south Texas in the fall of 1890 could never be sure when he would need all the power that a good horse could offer him. Mexican bandits, border outlaws, and small bands of roving renegade Indians remained a threat in the harsh country where the Croly County sheriff was headed. He intended to be prepared for whatever dangers he might face in the days before him.

In less than an hour, Wheeler reined up before the Wallaceville Drink Emporium to climb down from the saddle and loop Jim's reins around the hitching post that fronted the small saloon. He reached out a hand to stroke the charcoal's neck while letting his eyes wander over the slowly awakening town. Even though Wallaceville supported the surrounding territory of Croly County, the little town was hardly more than a village. The small collection of weathered buildings included a blacksmith shop and stable, owned by the feisty old Dooley Fisher, a meeting house that served as both church and school, a bank, a general store operated by Oscar Wilhite, and the Emporium presided over by Charlie Kuehnle.

'Mornin', Wheeler. Coffee's hot and black.' Wheeler pushed through the batwing doors of the little saloon to be greeted by the barkeep who placed a mug of steaming brew on the scarred counter before him. The bartender was fiftyish, bald, plump, and stood all of five feet and four inches in height. His face was clean-shaven except for a tuft of grey hair that sprouted from below his lower lip. A clean, fresh apron covered the saloon owner's attire. He leaned an elbow upon the bar and sipped the steaming black liquid from his own mug as Wheeler crossed the sawdust covered floor from the doorway.

'Good mornin', Charlie,' Wheeler grinned and waved a hand in greeting. His hazel eyes surveyed the room. The Emporium held a dozen or so large round tables with red and white checkered tablecloths. A rough wooden bar ran the length of the room with space for another dozen customers. Posters and advertisements filled the walls until no wood seemed to show; no one knew how many layers of cardboard advertising Charlie had managed to accumulate on his walls over the twenty years he had been in business.

'What brings you to town this early in the mornin'?' Charlie's place was the centre of local gossip, due in no small part to the owner's active participation in this dubious pastime. 'Everything all right out to the Bar W?'

'Everything's fine, Charlie,' Wheeler sipped the coffee before continuing, 'just need to pick up a few supplies before I take a little trip down south.' The part-time sheriff explained all about Carlos Mendoza's visit the night before. 'I'll be gone at least a couple of weeks.'

'Sounds like this could be dangerous...' the barkeep never finished the thought, for Darlene, a frumpy middle-aged blonde, pushed through the kitchen door with two plates heaped high with eggs, ham, and biscuits.

'I thought I heard you out here, Wheeler McKay,' Darlene greeted the peace officer. 'I don't care where you're headed, you got time for some breakfast before you go. Odel and I ain't gonna let you take off from here without a full belly.' Odel, Darlene's husband, worked the grill out back while Darlene waited tables. They were as much a part of the Emporium as old Charlie himself.

'Thanks, Darlene,' Wheeler called out, but the woman was already disappearing into the kitchen to help her husband with preparations for the long day ahead. Conversation was suspended while the two men ate their breakfast with enthusiasm.

After wiping his mouth with a ragged square of cloth provided for the purpose, Wheeler took a final sip of lukewarm coffee that drained the mug.

'You reckon Oscar's up yet?' he asked of the barkeep.

'Sure, he's up,' Charlie answered with a mischievous grin, 'and if he ain't, then he ought to be. Just bang on the front door; anybody lying in bed this time a mornin' deserves to be rousted out.'

'Take it easy,' the young man called out as he left the friendly bar to step out into the bright sunlight. It was a beautiful day with blue, cloudless skies and crisp, cool air; a fine day for the long ride ahead.

'Take care!' The barkeep raised his voice to be heard by the figure retreating from the Emporium doors. Concern etched the man's pudgy face and wrinkled his brow.

In fact, Oscar Wilhite was open for business. Wheeler McKay was able to purchase the few supplies he needed for his journey to the border. He filled the saddle bags with goods. He had coffee, flour, some canned peaches, extra shells for the Colt .45 and Winchester rifle, along with a variety of odds and ends. Two full canteens of water and an extra blanket completed the light load he would take along. He pulled himself into the saddle and nudged Jim to a walk as he exited Wallaceville down the town's Main Street. Passing Dooley Fisher's stable, he turned the big black south and west.

He had travelled only a short distance down the dusty trail when he rounded a bend to find a familiar figure seated beneath the branches of a large oak tree. A big bay horse stood patiently beside the man. Wheeler slowed Jim as he approached the big man. A curious gleam came to the lawman's hazel eyes as he watched the giant rise to his feet beneath the gnarled old tree.

'I've been waitin' on you, Mr McKay.' Abe Davis stood tall as Wheeler brought his horse to a halt along the side of the narrow road. 'I'm ready to ride. Bullwhip and the others can handle the Bar W while we're away. Work's a little slow 'bout now anyway.'

'I don't follow you, Abe, what've you got in mind?' Wheeler's puzzled expression evidenced his confusion over the presence of the big, black ranch hand who towered before him. He searched the handsome face for answers.

'I'm goin' with you.' The man's brown eyes met and held the gaze of Wheeler McKay. 'You can't do this alone and I'm comin' along to help. It's as simple as that.' Abe put a boot in the stirrup and pulled himself into the bay's worn saddle.

'I appreciate the offer, Abe,' Wheeler's tone was pleasant but firm, 'but I can't ask you to do it. This could be serious business and I can't ask any man to risk his life for any...'

'You didn't ask, Mr McKay,' Abe interrupted, 'and really, there's nothin' you can do to stop me.' He smiled showing even white teeth. 'Now, are we goin' to Grandview to help them folks or not?'

Wheeler took a moment to appraise the big man who sat his horse beside him along the trail. He noticed for the first time that, in addition to the man's usual jeans, boots, and red plaid shirt, Abe now carried a Remington Frontier .44 holstered at his right hip along with an old Winchester .44 in a worn saddle sheath. His hazel eyes met the dark, determined gaze of the other as a long silence stretched the seconds into eternities.

'Can you use those weapons?' Wheeler asked.

'They're not for show,' Abe grinned but his brown eyes grew serious. 'When the time comes, you won't have to look out for me. I'll be right beside you with a gun in my hand.'

'We're wastin' time here,' Wheeler smiled. 'Let's ride.'

The two men touched heels to horses and set off along the dusty road for Grandview.

Mid-day found the two men stopped in the

shade of a small clump of trees. Letting the horses rest, Wheeler and Abe sat quietly for long minutes as they enjoyed the small snack of cold ham and biscuit from the charcoal's saddle bags; washing it down with a few swallows of cool water. Wheeler had removed the heavy buckskin coat to wrap it in the blanket roll tied behind his saddle. The day had warmed as the sun climbed high and now the travellers enjoyed the slight breeze that stirred the dry, colourful leaves clinging to the branches above their heads.

'Why are you comin' along, Abe?' Wheeler broke the silence as he replaced the cap upon his canteen. 'Why run the risk?'

'I could ask you the same ting.' Abe's deep bass voice carried power and conviction.

'Carlos Mendoza is a friend of mine. He came to me for help and...'

'That's not all of it and you know it,' Abe interrupted his Bar W boss. 'That's not the half of it. We're goin' down to Grandview to help those poor Mexican peasants out from under that town boss, Big Jake Hollister.'

Wheeler started to speak but the other man continued. 'This is more than helping out a friend. We're goin' to that bordertown hell-hole to overthrow a tyrant. It's a job nobody else will do. So, it's up to us.'

'But why, Abe?' Wheeler persisted. 'You might be killed for a town full of people you don't even know.'

'Just the same as you, Mr McKay.' Abe flashed another grin then quickly sobered. 'I know about oppression. I know all about people who are used and beaten, Mr McKay. I was born in Mississippi just after the war. My parents had been slaves before that war, and they named me for the president who set them free. They learned to read and write and they made sure that I learned too. Life was tough for a black family in Mississippi after the war, but Mamma and Papa sent me away to school in Alabama.' The big man shook his head slowly and stared down at the earth. 'It was while I was away at school that it happened. We had a small farm; just a few acres to scratch out a living from the dirt.

Three years ago night-ridin' Klan came to my family's home to murder and burn. There was nothin' left when they finished. The county claimed back taxes and confiscated our land. I left school and drifted west lookin' for some place where I could find peace and some measure of real freedom. I found that at the Bar W with your family and ranch hands.'

'I'm glad to hear that,' Wheeler spoke quietly. 'You know my father fought in that war, Abe, and I wear the hat that his commanding officer gave him when it all ended.' He paused and waited for the other man to meet his gaze. 'That doesn't mean that I believe in the old cause. I hope you understand. I wear this hat out of respect for my father, not out of some old set of hatreds and prejudices.'

'I know,' Abe nodded solemnly. 'I wouldn't be here if I didn't know that. I almost rode on down the trail when I first came across the Bar W; all because of that old Confederate hat you wear.' He gave Wheeler an infectious grin. 'I'm glad I didn't. The past few months with the Wallace family and the Bar W crew have taught me something I never really understood until now.'

'What's that? Wheeler gave his companion a curious look.

'All white folks ain't bad,' the big man asserted. 'In fact, the best I can tell, you all are just about the same as us, with enough good and bad to go around for all races. Now, we got a fight on our hands, Mr McKay, and it's my turn to help somebody out from under oppression. I don't plan on missin' out on this opportunity any more than you do.'

'I understand, Abe,' Wheeler replied softly, then shifted the mood of the conversation. 'There's only one thing we've got to get straight if we're goin' to ride all the way to the Mexican border and back together.'

'What's that, Mr McKay?'

'Drop the "mister"!' Wheeler rose to his feet to stick out his hand in the direction of the other man. 'If we're in this thing together, then call me "Wheeler" just like I've been askin' you for the past three months.' He smiled as the big man grabbed his hand and Wheeler pulled him to his feet. They paused for a brief moment of silent camaraderie.

'That'll be just fine, Wheeler.' Abe returned his partner's grin before each man turned away to mount the horses who stood by patiently in the cooling shade.

Side by side, the two Bar W cowboys resumed a steady pace along the trail to Grandview. The powerful animals stretched their legs while eating up the miles that separated them from an inevitable showdown with Big Jake Hollister.

FOUR

Darkness found Wheeler and Abe settled comfortably around a small fire along the trail that led to Grandview. The cool fall air made the little blaze all the more appealing as the two men sat, using saddles for back-rests, listening to the night sounds as they enjoyed a final cup of coffee to complete their evening meal.

'One of us will have to scare up some game tomorrow,' Wheeler commented idly before sipping another mouthful of the hot, black brew.

'A long-eared Texas jack-rabbit would make for a good stew. I even brought along a few potatoes and carrots from the Bar W garden.' Abe's wide grin sparkled in the fire-light. 'If we've got to travel hard then we might as well travel with full stomachs.

The men were quiet for several minutes; each absorbed with his own thoughts. It had been a long day of travel with the hardest part of their journey still before them. After that, their troubles really began.

'Who do you reckon is out there?' Abe broke the silence after draining the coffee from his tin mug.

'I don't know but they've been with us most of the day.' Wheeler shifted the old Confederate hat to the back of his head before meeting the brown eyes that searched his face.

'I first saw we were being followed just after we stopped for that rest around lunch time.' Abe adjusted his big frame in an effort to find a soft spot upon the rocky earth beneath him. 'I could tell that you've been watchin' our back trail all afternoon.'

'Whoever it is,' Wheeler observed, 'had to set out after us from somewhere around Wallaceville. Could be that Jake Hollister found out about that letter to Carlos and sent some company along to stop it from

70

reaching the old man.'

'Or to stop anybody from interfering in his business just in case it did reach him,' Abe interjected solemnly.

'That too, Abe,' Wheeler was thoughtful, 'that too.'

'You want to take turns at watch tonight? I can take the first shift and let you get some shut-eye.'

'No,' Wheeler shook his head in the fading yellow light of the camp fire. 'If trouble comes, Jim'll wake us up. He's a light sleeper, and we can both use a good night's rest.' He pulled a sturdy, blue wool blanket over his powerful form before slumping down to stretch out upon the ground. Resting his head upon the saddle, he pulled the hat down over his eyes. 'Tomorrow we've got to find out just who that is behind us. We got enough trouble without waitin' out a surprise from an uninvited guest.'

Before long, soft snores mingled with the crackling, snapping noises of the dying fire and the night time sounds that surrounded

71

the little campsite. Two tired men slept without dreams.

Abe awakened instantly at the first touch of fingers upon his shoulder. The big man sat up with the Remington .44 in his right fist.

'Hold on partner; it's just me.'

'Wheeler! I could've blown your head off.' Abe lowered the pistol to glare at the figure crouched nearby in the inky blackness. 'What do you want at this time of the mornin'?' He surveyed the night sky. 'It must be two or three hours before first light.'

'I'd say you're right.' Wheeler rose to his feet to cross the little campsite. Standing before his saddle gear, he began his brief explanation, 'I've got plans for our visitor.' He pulled the Winchester .44-40 from the saddle scabbard. 'Whoever it is following us is probably pretty close behind along the trail. He has no reason to believe that we know he's there, and should be sound asleep by now.'

'Yeah, like anybody with good sense would

be at this hour of the mornin',' Abe grumbled good-naturedly as he stood up and strapped the gunbelt around his waist. 'So, what have you got in mind?'

'I'll head back down the trail on foot until I come on the campsite of the owlhoot that's followin' us.' He paused a moment to settle the battered grey hat upon his brown hair. 'You follow along just a few minutes behind me as a back-up. If anything happens to me, then it's your job to pull the fat out of the fire. Between the two of us we ought to be able to take this man by surprise and get the story on why he's here. That sound okay with you?'

'What're you waitin' on?' Abe pulled his old Winchester .44 from the saddle boot that lay nearby. 'I'll be right behind you.'

The Croly County lawman vanished down the trail into the night without making another sound. He moved softly through the darkness making no noise along the well-packed trail they had followed earlier that day. Holding the saddle-gun in his hands ready for action, Wheeler made rapid progress, knowing that Abe would be following close behind within a matter of minutes. He felt a sense of confidence in the giant Bar W cowhand even though he had known the man only a few short months.

A little more than half an hour had passed when he saw the faint glow of orange embers from a fading fire. Wheeler slowed his pace to approach the campsite in silence. With great caution, he took up a position nearby to survey the small clearing where last night's blaze had become no more than a pile of smouldering wood.

Close to the remnants of that fire lay a blanket roll. The form beneath the rumpled covers gave no indication of movement as he watched from behind a lone sweetgum tree. He assumed the figure to be soundly sleeping in the pre-dawn darkness of early morning. Off in the darkness, on the far side of the camp, stood a lone horse that occasionally shuffled dry leaves as it shifted about in the still, quiet black of night. Unconcerned with the horse, Wheeler returned his attention to the huddled form underneath the blanket. A few more moments of observation, just to be certain, and he would make a move to clear up this minor mystery once and for all.

Cautiously leaving the cover of the tree behind him, Wheeler silently crept to within ten feet of the bedroll. He lined the rifle upon the midsection of the heavy blanket before barking out a challenge that would wake the dead.

'Rise and shine, mister!' His voice exploded in the still, night air. 'You've got some explainin' to do!'

The form never moved. Wheeler knew instantly that he had been suckered by one of the oldest tricks in the book.

'Buenos noches!' A familiar voice called from behind him. 'It is not so easy to catch an old man napping, is it young one?'

Wheeler turned in time to see Carlos Mendoza step out of the surrounding darkness from behind a gnarled, old oak. The slender man carried an old American Arms 12-gauge shotgun with barrels sawed off for close range work. Around his waist was an ornate cartridge belt with a Remington Army .44 riding high on his right hip. Otherwise, the elderly Mexican servant from the Circle D appeared as always in white shirt, black pants, and high-heeled western boots.

'The eyes are not all that they used to be, *mi amigo.*' Carlos shook his head before offering up a wink. 'But with this,' he held up the shotgun with the short, stubby barrels, 'excellent vision is of little importance.'

Wheeler found himself unable to speak for a few moments. When he did collect his thoughts and find his voice, it was to shout into the night.

'Come on in, Abe!'

'Right here.' The big man stepped into the faint glow from the remaining embers with the Winchester cradled in his arms. 'Looks like we found our man.'

'I am flattered,' Carlos grinned. 'You gentlemen must have expected one very tough hombre.'

'Carlos,' Wheeler turned now to face the elderly Mexican with obvious irritation in his voice, 'this is no joke. Just what do you think you're doing here?'

'You did not really think that I would allow you to go to Grandview alone did you?' The old man's steely eyes bored into Wheeler's. 'Did you think that I would let you fight a battle for my people and for my family without me? It is right that I come along.'

'You're too old for this, Carlos,' Wheeler insisted. 'Someone could be hurt.' He paused for a long moment before continuing. 'Some-one could even be killed. You must go home as soon as it's light.'

'*Si si,*' Carlos grinned, 'this old dog is much too feeble to catch the young pup who slips up in the dark of night.'

Abe's chuckle came out as a muted rumble from deep in his chest while the Mexican's smile flashed white teeth that reflected the camp fire's remaining glow.

'You could help me here anytime now.'

Wheeler spoke sharply to his large companion.

'Oh I think you're doin' fine, Wheeler,' Abe brought his laughter under control. 'Just remind him one more time about how he's too old to go along with us.'

Even Wheeler could not repress a grin at the giant's sarcastic remark. Before long, all three men were laughing as they gathered up the old man's gear and prepared to saddle his spirited pinto pony. By afternoon, the three men were deep into south west Texas. The terrain had changed from sparse woods and meadows to rocky, rugged flatland with scattered brush and scrubby, stunted trees.

It had quickly become clear to Wheeler that Carlos Mendoza would not return to the Circle D voluntarily, and that there was really no way to force the elderly gentleman's retreat from the journey to Grandview. Therefore, the decision had been an easy one. Carlos would come along in order to visit his niece, Juanita Alvarez, but would stay out of trouble. The young peace officer only hoped that the old man would hold up his end of the bargain. He and Abe would have their hands full once they hit the Mexican border. They really could not afford the time to look out after a white-haired old hellion as well.

The sound of distant gunfire brought the trio up short. Wheeler raised a hand calling them to a halt upon the dusty trail. Motioning for silence, he listened to the sharp crack of a rifle, followed by the whine of lead ricocheting from rock to rock. Other shots sounded, spaced at intervals of several seconds, and then a sustained burst of seven shots in a row echoed out across the countryside.

'Sounds like a small battle goin' on up ahead,' Abe voiced the obvious and Carlos nodded his head in agreement.

'Let's go real slow.' Wheeler's tone remained calm. 'We should be able to get a good look at things from atop this next rise.'

They walked the horses a few hundred

yards before dismounting to cautiously approach the edge of the gently-sloping incline. On the other side of the hill's peak the ground abruptly dropped away at a sharp angle, falling off some fifteen feet of steeply-sloping ground. Belly down atop the small bluff, the three men could see out across the rolling flat land before them. Another two hundred yards distance and they found the source of the gunshots. As Abe had indicated, a minor battle had erupted along the rugged trail to Grandview.

A small depression, littered with rocks and boulders had become a temporary fortress for a lone man and his buckskin pony. The horse stood quietly in a natural stone enclosure while the man hunkered down between two boulders with a rifle in his hands. As the trio watched, he snapped off a quick shot. His efforts brought a volley from scattered sources before him. Lead whined off the rocks as the lone figure scrunched himself into a tight ball behind the rocky shelter he had found in this south Texas wasteland.

'You think we'd be jumpin' the gun if we were to help this man out?' Abe asked quietly.

'No,' Wheeler replied, 'looks to me as if he could use a little help about now.'

'You reckon those others are bandits?'

'That's the way I got it figgered. *Bandidos* from Mexico; they slip across the border in small groups to ambush unsuspecting travellers.' He paused a moment before shifting a glance toward the old man. 'What do you think, Carlos?'

'*Si*,' the white head nodded with conviction, '*son bandidos.*'

'All right then.' Wheeler carefully surveyed the scene before him. 'There appears to be four of them from what I can see. Two are seventy yards directly in front of our new friend's hideaway, and each of the others is attempting to circle around to get at him from the sides. He's pinned down good. If we don't act quickly they'll have him surrounded for sure.'

'That looks about right to me.' Abe began

to move away from the ridge in the direction of the horse. 'I suggest that you take the one on the left and I'll go to the right.' He managed a grim smile. 'We can share the two in the middle.'

Wheeler nodded his assent as he pulled himself into the saddle upon the big charcoal's back. Jim shifted beneath his master's weight, sensing the tension that filled the air.

'Carlos.' The lawman's voice carried a note of warning. 'You keep your head low and bring up the rear only if we really need you.'

'At your service.' The old man bowed from the waist. His eyes twinkled as they met Abe's. Both men understood the limitations of the old man's compliance.

Abe and Wheeler touched heels to their mounts for a burst of speed that took them over the ridge and down the steep embankment in a flash. Within seconds, the two riders streaked across the rugged flatland at a full gallop. They covered the two hundred yards in such a short time that the bandits had no time to prepare a response. Too late, the bushwhackers opened fire. Almost in the same instant, Abe and Wheeler brought their horses to a halt as they leaped from the saddles to confront the outlaws attempting to circle the man pinned behind the boulders.

The Peacemaker in his fist, Wheeler spotted a leering head some twenty yards before him. The man triggered a shot that crackled past Wheeler's ear then ducked behind the stone outcropping for cover. Hearing the man's boots scuffling about, the Bar W rancher waited long seconds for the oily head to appear once more. Soon, head and shoulders popped into view from a different location. The Colt .45 boomed once. The head exploded in a crimson spray. Wheeler quickly advanced to the small cluster of rocks that had sheltered the bandit. The man now lay dead in the Texas sun while a swarm of blue flies discovered an unexpected feast.

Meanwhile, Abe had managed to take his

man without complications. Leaping from the saddle, the giant had discovered he had misjudged his distances. This miscalculation had brought him to within thirty feet of his target, another Mexican outlaw with cartridge belts cross his shallow chest. The obviously frightened bandit had been caught in the process of scurrying back to his companions in an effort to escape the big man on the powerful bay. Now, faced by the towering form of Abraham Lincoln Davis, the rat-faced figure brought up a battered old Starr .44 level with Abe's midsection. He never fired.

As Abe left the saddle, he spotted the man who had darted behind a clump of scrubby brush. His sharp eyes caught the movement of the figure's right hand even as his own flashed downward to grasp the Remington .44 holstered at his right hip. A blur brought the pistol to bear upon his target and the gun sounded twice. The impact of the lead knocked the scrawny outlaw to the ground some five yards back, where he crumpled into a lifeless heap. Scarlet stained the hard earth beneath his still form as Abe found cover behind a small collection of nearby boulders. He waited for his partner's next move.

He did not have long to wait. Wheeler opened fire upon the remaining two bandits. Almost immediately he was joined by the rifles of Abe and the unknown man who had been pinned in the natural stone fortress. Shots rang out for a full minute then, as if on signal, abruptly ceased.

Within moments, the outlaws were mounted. The remaining pair of Mexican bandits used flashing silver spurs to urge their mounts away from the battle scene. The ambush had gone sour. Two of their gang were dead and the odds were now against them. The price for loot was too high on this day. Horses thundered south toward the border.

'Looks like it's over!' Wheeler shouted out to his companions. Then to the man behind the boulders. 'You mind if we come on in?'

'Come ahead!' The response sounded loud and clear.

The whole thing had only taken a few minutes. However, the sun had already begun to sink beneath the horizon and Wheeler figured that this natural shelter would be as good a place as any to camp the night. He waited until he saw Carlos join his little pinto pony with Abe's big bay, then moved out to meet the two as they advanced to the stone fortress and its occupant.

As they approached, the man stepped out from the rocks with a Henry .44 in his left hand. The right hovered near a short-barrelled Colt .45 that rode low; tied down to his right thigh with a rawhide thong. He stood just under six feet tall and would weigh in at a solid one hundred and seventy pounds of well-formed muscle. He was dressed in dark, dusty grey shirt stuffed into the pants, and a flat-crowned, black Stetson covering curly raven-black hair.

The face was long and lean, with high cheek bones, a crooked hawk nose, and deep-set green eyes. Black stubble sketched a square, dimpled chin and a small, thin-lipped mouth completed the man's features. It was a hard face with leather-tough, sun-bronzed skin. The stranger showed no emotion as the trio closed the gap across the rugged terrain.

'Much obliged,' the hard man's tone was flat. 'I'm glad you folks happened along when you did. Seems I found myself in what you might call a difficult situation.

'We couldn't just pass by and leave you to the bandits,' Wheeler answered the man with a smile.

'No.' The face evidenced no expression. 'I don't suppose you could at that.'

'Name's Wheeler McKay,' the young man spoke up as the verbal exchange wound down to an uncomfortable silence. 'This here is Abe Davis and Carlos Mendoza.' He indicated his companions and each nodded in turn as the hard man shifted his eyes from face to face.

'We're from up around Wallaceville in

Croly County,' Wheeler continued with no encouragement, 'on our way down to Grandview along the Mexican border.'

For a brief moment, mild surprise registered in the stranger's river-green eyes. He let an expectant silence elapse before resuming the conversation.

'Good to meet you, gentlemen. I'm Chester Alison and I suppose we might as well travel along together from here.'

The trio looked upon the hard man with curious stares.

'I was on the way to Grandview myself when I got bushwhacked by them Mexican desperados. I got business in that little bordertown.' He paused briefly to scratch a match and hold it to the top of a thin, black cigar he had removed from his shirt pocket. After puffing the tobacco to life he flipped the match into the dirt at his feet and spoke again in that flat voice. 'I hear tell that Big Jake Hollister is hiring on hands and I aim to be one of 'em.'

FIVE

'There she is, gentlemen.' Wheeler McKay lifted an arm to point toward a small cluster of buildings on the distant horizon. The four men had brought their tired mounts to a halt upon sighting the bordertown of Grandview. Scrub brush and wiry, wild grasses cluttered the flat, sandy country that stretched out before them while a bright, blue cloudless sky appeared solid enough to touch.

'The view don't appear so grand to me,' Abe Davis commented dryly. Indeed, this arid south west corner of Texas had a harsh, barren quality that almost challenged the very existence of life itself. Whatever else Jake Hollister might be, Abe considered silently, he must be a man of great determination to build his Box H ranch in country such as this.

'It has been a long, long time.' Carlos Mendoza spoke in almost reverent tones while Chester Alison simply looked on in an emotionless silence.

Two days had passed since the three men had rescued the hard man from the hands of Mexican bandits along the trail to Grandview. In that time, Alison had contributed very little to the conversations but had, from time to time, offered up bits and pieces of his background. In his mid-forties, the gunman had worked at jobs ranging from cow puncher to town marshal and all stops in between. For the past several years he had drifted from job to job, relying, for the most part, upon his skill with the deadly Colt .45 carried low on his right hip. He had learned of Hollister's outfit while on a job up in southern Colorado. It sounded like steady, long-term work so he had drifted south with hopes of employment. The trio from Croly County had given no hint of their reasons for visiting the bordertown and Alison had never asked.

Now, the four horses plodded steadily toward the small town of Grandview. It had been a hard trip; both men and animals were near exhaustion. Gritty sand had found its way into the folds and crevices of their clothing, and they were covered with the dust of a long journey.

Approaching the outskirts of town, Wheeler's hazel eyes surveyed the grey, weathered structures that passed for local civilisation. He found the usual collection of businesses and offices in place, including a saloon, a marshal's office, a general store, a blacksmith shop and stable, a small community bank, and a half dozen frame houses. Then, still further out, several dozen adobe boxes that made up the Mexican community of Grandview. These homes set apart from the remainder of the village while hugging the border of their inhabitants' homeland.

In the midst of the town's business district, directly across from the saloon, stood a large, two-storey frame house painted a bright canary yellow with spring-green shutters and trim. Surrounded by drab grey, the clean sparkle and fresh colour of the big house drew the attention of the four men who directed their mounts up the main street toward the big livery barn.

They brought their horses to a halt before the stable. Each stepped down from the saddle in a stiff, hesitant manner, spending a few moments stretching muscles and flexing joints. The long ride to the Mexican border had taken a heavy toll upon them all. Fatigue enveloped the little group without exception.

'Afternoon.' A broad-shouldered man of fifty stepped into the sunlight through the wide stable doors. 'What can I do for you fellers?' Standing six feet in height and carrying well over two hundred pounds upon his large frame, the big man's bald head glowed bronze in the bright sunlight. Bushy, iron-grey chin whiskers hung to his chest while small brown eyes and a bulbous nose settled under wild eyebrows that stuck out in all directions. Sail-like ears completed the man's features. He wore brown canvas pants tucked into high-topped boots and an open-collared, plaid shirt with sleeves rolled up to bare his massive forearms. 'I'm Silas Weaver. I own this livery.'

'Mr Weaver,' Wheeler closed the gap that separated them while reaching out his hand to grasp the big paw offered by the livery man, 'it's a pleasure to meet you. I'm Wheeler McKay. This here is Abe Davis, Carlos Mendoza, and Chester Alison. We'd be obliged if you could find room for our horses for a few days.'

'That's my business, folks,' the man's tone was gruff but without malice. 'I'll give 'em good care and stow your gear. They'll be here when you're ready to leave. I live over the stable so's you can get me anytime of the day or night. Just bang on the doors if I've locked up.'

'We appreciate that, Mr Weaver.' Wheeler's manner was polite and conversational.

'I could make you a fine offer on that charcoal,' Weaver observed as he took the big stallion's reins.

'No, thank you, he's not for sale.'

'I'm not surprised,' the livery man grumbled. 'A fine animal such as that rarely is.'

'Hollister.' Chester Alison spoke now for the first time in his flat, expressionless voice. His eyes fixed upon the stable owner's face with a cold, hard stare. 'I'm lookin' fer Big Jake Hollister.'

'Yes, sir,' Weaver looked away from the gunman's gaze. 'Just knock on that green door at the big yaller house. If Mr Hollister ain't there then whoever answers that door will surely get in touch with him right away.'

Silas Weaver quickly led the horses into the cool shadows of the big barn leaving the four men in the dusty street outside. An awkward silence gripped the four for a brief moment as each stood holding saddle bags and long guns with the Texas sun high over-head.

'Well, I guess this is where we part company for a while,' Wheeler smiled in the direction of Alison. 'I suppose we'll see you around town here and there; maybe have a drink or two one evenin'.'

'I reckon so,' Alison replied. Without another word he hoisted his saddle bags to rest upon his left shoulder then set off down the street in the direction of the immaculate yellow house.

'I must go and find my niece, *mi amigos*,' Carlos smiled. Of them all, Carlos seemed the least depleted by the long hours in the saddle. In fact, the slender, white haired gentleman seemed refreshed by the prospects of locating his niece. The old man was obviously happy to be in Grandview, and looking forward to a small reunion with a small portion of his family. Even under these dangerous circumstances, it would be good to be with his people once again after so many years among the *Americanos* of Croly County.

'We'll catch up to you later, Carlos,' Wheeler assured his companion. 'Abe and I will find a room and get cleaned up. Let's meet later for dinner. You go hunt up your niece and the local *cantina*.'

'*Si,*' Carlos called hastily over his shoulder as he took long, rapid strides away from his friends. '*Adios.*'

'Goodbye,' both men called as the man disappeared in the direction of the adobe huts that constituted the area of town where the Mexican population lived. They had no doubt that Carlos would quickly locate his niece, along with a suitable spot for dinner and refreshments.

'Let's find a room and a bath.' Wheeler set off in the direction of the large saloon that fronted Main Street. It was, apparently, the only such establishment in town and carried no name except for the identifying weathered lettering 'Saloon and Hotel' painted across the two-storey building's grey board front. Abe kept pace as they neared the unimposing structure.

They made an unusual duo plodding down the dusty street that sliced through the town. The Croly County lawman possessed a powerful frame and rugged good looks but the handsome black man towered over him. The task ahead lay heavy upon their minds as Abe and Wheeler pushed through the batwing doors and entered the local centre for drinks, food, entertainment, and lodging.

The barroom was big. Two dozen or more tables were scattered about the sawdust-covered floor while a long mahogany bar ran the length of the far wall. A large, gilt-edged mirror covered the wall behind the counter and gaudy paintings of scantily clad women decorated the three remaining surfaces. Two girls in colourful, low cut gowns sat with three men at one of the tables, but otherwise the saloon remained deserted in the middle of the afternoon. Wheeler gave them a glance as he stood inside the doors letting his eyes adjust to the interior gloom. He then crossed the floor to stand at the bar with Abe following close behind.

'I'll have a beer, please,' Wheeler dropped a coin upon the bar as he met the bartender's wary gaze. The barkeep was a little man, about five feet tall, with thin, black hair plastered across his skull. A gaunt face and shrivelled features made the man look old, although he was only about fifty-five. He could weigh no more than an even hundred pounds soaking wet and fully clothed. The little man wiped his hands upon a once white apron as he approached his new customers with obvious reluctance.

'You want a beer, Abe?' Wheeler asked.

'Count me in.' The giant kept his back to the bar and let his brown eyes wander around the room. In towns of this size, the local saloon often doubled as a hotel as well.

In seconds, the bartender set two mugs of tepid beer before the men and collected the coin from the counter top. He had not yet spoken when he turned to shuffle off toward the cigar box where he kept the bar receipts.

'We need a room for a few nights,' Wheeler kept his tone conversational in spite of the bartender's surly attitude. The man from Wallaceville made it a habit to be polite until he was overtly provoked.

'Ain't got no room,' the little man called over his shoulder as he dropped the coin into the box. 'We're all filled up.' He flashed Wheeler a squinty-eyed look before shifting his eyes to the broad back of the big man who stood beside him at the bar.

'Sign out front says you rent rooms.' Wheeler sipped at the warm beer. 'We need a place to stay.'

'I told you, I ain't got no...'

'I heard you the first time,' Wheeler's voice took on a hard, cold edge, 'and I told you that we need a room.'

'We don't rent no rooms to coloureds, mister,' the man's shrivelled lips curled into a snarl. 'He'll have to sleep over the barn with the other animals.'

Abe tensed momentarily but then forced himself to relax. He had been through this before and knew not to let his emotions drive his thinking. Instead, the giant continued to rest his elbows upon the bar in order to keep the big room under surveillance. The three cowboys had ceased flirting with the bar girls, and had fallen silent as the conversation at the bar attracted their attention.

Wheeler carefully set the half empty mug back on the counter before turning his hazel eyes upon the weasel-faced little man behind the bar. The wrinkled barkeep met the gaze momentarily then shivered before turning away to wipe at the mahogany surface with a stained rag.

'Now, I'm gonna pretend that I misunderstood you,' Wheeler's voice dropped low. His words were barely audible but the tone was deadly serious. 'You'll rent us a room and you'll have somebody bring up hot water for a couple of baths. Do we understand one another?'

'Yes, sir,' the withered lips managed to croak out a response before he scurried over to a box to extract a key. 'You'll be in Room 211. That's the best room in the house; a corner room with cross ventilation. That hot water will be right up.' The bartender never met Wheeler's eyes again, but turned his attention to stocking a shelf with clean glasses.

'Much obliged.' Wheeler dropped a wrinkled bill upon the counter to cover the costs of the room and baths. He and Abe stepped away from the bar to move in the direction of the steep, narrow stairs that led to the hotel rooms.

'Here it comes,' Abe whispered softly so that only his companion could hear.

'Hold up there, boy!' A harsh voice growled through the quiet of the barroom. 'Just where in hell do you think you're goin'?'

Abe and Wheeler turned in time to see the three men rising to their feet. The one who had spoken stood over six feet in height with two hundred pounds of bone and muscle distributed about his lanky frame. A square face and a strong jaw were topped by curly brown hair. His two companions were non-descript range hands of moderate height and weight. All three dressed in worn, faded and patched cowboy attire with scuffed, down-at-the-heel cattleman's boots. Each of the trio was in desperate need of a hot bath and clean clothes.

'We're goin' to our room.' Wheeler sounded calm and assured as the three hardcase cowboys approached them. 'We need a bath and a change of clothes. It's been a long trip and a dusty trail.'

'I ain't talkin' to you,' snarled the trio's spokesman, now standing a few feet away, 'I asked this here boy where he was goin'.'

'Just goin' to my room, mister.' Abe's voice carried no challenge but no submission. 'I don't want no trouble. I'm just looking for a place to stay and a good hot bath.'

'Well, well, well,' grinned the lanky cowboy, showing off crooked, yellow teeth, 'you done found trouble, boy. Now, you just turn yourself around and head right back out them doors before we...'

Abe knew what was coming so decided not to delay the conflict any longer. He took two quick steps forward to launch a powerful right cross that landed on the end of a stubbly chin. One of the smaller cow hands collapsed in a heap five feet away. He never twitched or moaned, but simply became a limp collection of limbs and soiled clothing. The other of the big man's companions moved toward Abe with a self-confident smirk as he let go a right of his own. Abe ducked beneath the clubbing fist but caught a left in the ear. That was all his opponent managed before the giant let loose a left uppercut that snapped back the other man's head. Quickly following through with a right-left combination to the head, Abe watched the man join his friend stretched out upon the sawdust floor. Immediately, Abe drew the big Remington Frontier .44 to cover the scrawny barkeep who had made a grab for the shotgun hidden below the counter. Seeing the pistol pointed at his chest, the shrivelled bartender lifted his hands above his head in resignation.

Meanwhile, the trio's leader had slipped a bone-handled knife from his boot before advancing upon Wheeler. A grim smile animated the young lawman's features as the tall cowboy approached him with the sharp steel in his dirty fist. In one swift move,

Wheeler's right hand darted to the hilt of the Bowie at his left hip while his right boot kicked out to connect with his opponent's right hand. The hard kick sent the other blade across the room and brought a curse from the lanky man who shook the damaged paw in pain and frustration.

'A knife is like a pistol,' Wheeler spoke with some amusement in his voice, 'you ought to know how to use it if you're gonna pull it.' In a flash of bright steel, Wheeler's Bowie darted forward to slice the buttons from the tall man's shirt. The big knife ended up with the needle point nestled beneath the man's blocky jaw. A small trickle of blood slid from a tiny prick in the man's skin while his eyes bulged from his skull in fear. The cowboy stood still as the moments ticked by with the knife point pressed evenly against the tender flesh beneath his chin.

'I'm even better with my pistol.' Wheeler removed the Bowie from the man's throat and wiped the small blood stain upon his opponent's shirt front before returning the blade to his beaded sheath. 'Now, we're gonna go upstairs and have that bath. I suggest that you tend to your partners here and keep your nose out of our business.'

Wheeler and Abe deliberately turned their backs to the lone cowboy and made their way up the stairs to find their assigned room. Below, the remaining cow puncher found a chair and sat down with a heavy sigh of relief. The barkeep crossed the floor with a bottle and glasses; both men quickly knocked back a shot of the amber liquid. Hands trembled as the two men replaced the empty glasses upon the table before them.

'We got to let Mr Hollister know about these fellers,' the big ranch hand spoke after wiping his mouth with the back of a calloused hand. 'These jaspers could be real trouble; ain't no doubt about it!'

The shrivelled bartender poured another round as they stared down at the still forms upon the barroom floor. Neither man had moved since falling to the big hard fists of Abe Davis. Sipping the second glass of whisky, the two men looked on and shook their heads in silence.

The evening meal found Abe and Wheeler seated at a small round table with Carlos and his niece, Juanita Alvarez. The bath and change of clothing had refreshed both men. Added to this was a meal of beans, tortillas, and hot chilli that brought tears to their eyes. Full of good food, the four companions now settled down to hot, black coffee and conversation.

'So,' Wheeler sat back after a sip of the thick, steaming liquid, 'tell us about Grandview and Big Jake Hollister.' His eyes wandered about the room as he spoke. The small *cantina* held no more than half a dozen tables. Scattered stubs of candles provided smoky illumination and made playful shadow patterns on the cracked adobe walls. A dozen diners filled the little room with muffled talk while Wheeler waited for Juanita to answer.

'*Senors,*' the beautiful young woman began, 'it is not a pretty story.' Juanita shook her head sadly. Her black hair shimmered in the flickering light of the candles as her face clouded over with sorrow. 'He has turned our village into a prison. Our people work for him in town and on his ranch, but receive very little pay. He owns the stores where he sells the things we need at a cost we cannot afford to pay. We owe him more and more money so we must work harder and harder to pay him back. His *gringo* gunmen force us to work for Big Jake. These men have beaten and killed our men and used our women.' A single tear slipped from the corner of her right eye to slide down her face. 'Several weeks ago I was almost caught by three of the Box H gun hands. I was able to escape, but not the man who rescued me. They beat and shot poor Paco to death in a back alley.' Her body trembled at the remembrance. 'This is a hell-town, senors, and the worst of the devils is Big Jake Hollister.'

'Has anyone tried to fight him?' Abe asked softly in the dim light of the tiny *cantina*.

'With what?' Carlos answered. 'These

people have no guns. They are poor and defenceless. What little they might have possessed, Jake Hollister has already taken from them. All they have now is their lives, and,' he looked into Wheeler's eyes as he completed the sentence, 'if we wait too long then my people will not even have this.'

Wheeler finished his coffee before replacing the mug upon the scarred surface of the table. Silence gripped the four as all eyes turned to the young sheriff from Wallaceville. Hope burned brightly in the eyes of Carlos and Juanita while cold determination seemed evident in the deep brown eyes of Abe Davis. He met each of their stares in turn before giving off a small shrug accompanied by a slight sigh. He winked a hazel eye at Abe before offering his companions a confident smile.

'We'll look around in the mornin',' he announced with calm assurance, 'but tonight we all need a good rest.'

SIX

Just after sunrise, Wheeler and Abe found ladderback chairs in a small café that fronted a dusty side road just off the town's main street. A half dozen small tables with stained checkered tablecloths were scattered about the room in no apparent pattern while a mixed assortment of scarred wooden chairs surrounded each of the tiny tables. Even at this early hour the little restaurant was beginning to fill with hungry patrons. The two Bar W cowboys had discovered seats in the far back corner enabling them to keep a careful eye upon the comings and goings as they enjoyed their breakfast.

Steaming mugs of thick, black coffee sat upon the table before the two ranch hands. Abe raised a chipped cup to his lips for a sip of the scalding brew while Wheeler looked on in amusement.

'You'd better just wait it out, Abe,' Wheeler observed. 'Ain't nothin' better than simple patience in matters such as this.' He offered his companion a good natured wink along with a friendly grin.

'I expect you might be right.' Abe replaced the mug upon the table before stretching his large, well-muscled frame in an effort to loosen joints gone stiff and sore from past days in the saddle. 'That night in a feather-bed sure 'nuff made these achy bones feel a sight better. I'm ready to meet the old devil himself now.'

'My guess is that we'll both have that op-portunity before too much longer.' Wheeler commented matter-of-factly as the waiter brought them two plates piled high with eggs, ham, and biscuits. Without another word, the two men began heaping the food into their mouths, enjoying their first real breakfast after the long days on the trail to Grandview.

'You see that man over by the door?' Abe

asked as he washed down a mouthful of eggs with a big gulp of coffee.

'I suppose you're talkin' about that fellow in the black that's been watchin' us for the past five minutes.' Wheeler smiled as he swallowed a mouthful of ham. He then reached for his own mug. 'Yes, I imagine Big Jake Hollister has his eye on us already.'

The two resumed eating under the close observation of the figure seated across the room. His lanky frame covered in black from head to toe, the man's presence screamed gunfighter. The flat-crowned, narrow-brimmed Stetson sported a silver concho band and bright shiny silver decorated his black leather vest and gunbelt as well. Two ebony handled Smith and Wesson Schofield .45 revolvers were worn about his hips with the butts forward for a fancy cross draw. Approaching fifty, the gunman's face was creased and lined with years of hard living, while the curly blond hair that spilled to his shoulders carried streaks of grey. Hard, dark eyes covered the remainder of his face. Big, ornate silver spurs completed the man's image.

As Abe and Wheeler finished their breakfast, the man in black rose to his feet. Conversation in the crowded café fell to a hushed whisper. The jingle of the man's spurs could be heard as he crossed the floor to approach the table in the far corner.

'You folks new aroun' these parts ain't ya?' The man had come to a stop a few feet away and offered up a squinty-eyed look accompanied by a scowl of displeasure.

'Yes,' Wheeler acknowledged the gunman. 'We just arrived in town yesterday afternoon. I'm Wheeler McKay and this is Abe Davis.'

'We ain't much on visitors 'round here.' The man's thumbs remained hooked into his gunbelt; his hands rested inches from the holstered pistols. 'Might be best if you boys was to jest move along. You know, pack on up and drift back to wherever you come from.'

'Are you the local law?' Wheeler asked in

his usual polite, conversational tone without any hint of irritation or challenge in his voice.

'Naw, son,' the man gave a wolf smile that would have frightened babies, 'let's jest say I'm the welcomin' committee.' As quickly as it appeared, the smile vanished as the eyes grew hard again. 'You're welcome to leave here jest as soon as you can get your horses saddled.'

'We thank you for your time,' Wheeler smiled broadly while Abe glared at the gunfighter with an expression of smouldering anger, 'but we really must be going. We've got matters to attend to this morning.' The Croly County lawman rose to his feet. Abe quickly followed his lead, digging into his pocket with his left hand for coins to cover the cost of the morning meal.

'I don't think you understand what I'm tellin' you two fellers.' The gunman standing before them shifted his stance; spacing his legs for stability. His fingers spread before him in preparation for a fast draw. 'I mean pack up, saddle up, and git out of town!'

'No thank you.' A faint smile remained frozen on Wheeler's lips as his hard hazel eyes met the stare of the older gunman. 'Now, if you'll excuse us, please.'

Without a moment's hesitation, the gunfighter's hands flashed to the holstered revolvers at his hips. The two pistols had just cleared leather when the black clad figure found himself looking down the long barrel of a Colt .45 Peacemaker. Shifting his gaze to the side, he was aware of Abe's big Remington pointed at his belt buckle. Letting the guns slip from his fingers back into the holsters, the shootist slowly raised his hands to shoulder height.

'Now, just who are you, mister, and who sent you to run us off?' Wheeler might have been engaged in a simple exchange of pleasantries on a sunny morning.

'Name's Elton Torrence and I work for Hollister.' The man's eyes began to cross as he looked down the big bore of the deadly .45. The black hole remained steady in a line between his dark, dangerous eyes.

'Well, Mr Torrence, I really don't want to kill you,' Wheeler spoke softly while the other customers sat in stunned silence. 'So, how 'bout if you unbuckle that gunbelt real easy now and gently place it on the table between us here.'

Torrence did as he was instructed, then once again lifted his hands to his shoulders. He locked his gaze with Wheeler's hazel eyes before speaking again.

'You're purty good.' Elton Torrence was relaxed now. 'Fact is, you're damn good! Truth to tell, you're not bad yourself either,' the gunfighter nodded in Abe's direction; his voice remained calm, steady, and composed. 'After some twenty-odd years in this business you're the first to beat me.' A slight grin animated his rugged features. 'Now, I might be slowin' down a bit, but I'm still better than most.' He paused a moment before meeting Wheeler's eyes again with a serious, questioning stare. 'What now, son? Where do we go from here?'

'That's up to you,' Wheeler responded, returning the gunman's gaze. 'I've already told you that I'd rather not have to kill you.' He let the statement hang for a moment then offered the shootist a smile. 'Any place you might need to go; some place far away from Grandview?'

'Damn straight there is, son!' A genuine look of relief brightened the creased leather of the gunfighter's face. 'I can be gone within the hour. There's places I ain't never been that need this old carcass a heap more than this dirty little bordertown.'

Wheeler scooped up the gunbelt from the table then looped it over his left shoulder. The man in black eyed the pistols with a question mark upon his face.

'I'll leave these for you at the saloon.' Wheeler nodded toward his recently-vacated chair. 'Why don't you have another cup of coffee before you leave.' The suggestion was more of a veiled command.

'Don't mind if I do.' Torrence moved to the chair where he quickly took a seat against the wall. 'By the way, I'd look out for Hollister. He owns most of this town, and he don't like strangers pokin' their noses into his business. You boys already stirred up enough trouble over to the saloon yesterday. He wants y'all out of town.'

'Thanks for the warnin',' Wheeler smiled as he dropped the Peacemaker back into his holster.

'One more thing,' the gunfighter's words stopped Wheeler as he turned to leave, 'you better keep a careful eye on Morgan Erskin. 'You're fast McKay, but Morgan is a professional, and he's as good as they come. He ain't like me neither. I'm the old breed, son. You beat me fair and square so I'll move on. Morgan'll use any dirty trick he can and then shoot you in the back if that don't work. Don't give him no chances, boy, cause he'll kill you quick as you'd stomp a Texas cockroach.'

'Goodbye, Mr Torrence.' Wheeler turned to cross the floor of the crowded cafe with all eyes upon him. Abe cautiously brought up the rear, backing his way toward the door with his brown eyes intently focused upon the lean, black-clad gunfighter. Abe's long, supple fingers remained close to the grip of his holstered Remington until he and Wheeler were safe in the narrow street before the eatery.

'You should've killed that man, Wheeler.' Abe's tone carried solid conviction. His eyes reflected the burning anger of his soul. 'He was gonna kill us and you should've put a bullet through his head while you had the chance.'

'No point to it, Abe. Elton Torrence won't trouble us again.' Wheeler's response brought only a scowl of disapproval from his companion as they set off down the road in the direction of Main Street.

After dropping off the gunman's belt and pistols at the saloon, the two men took a casual stroll about town. As Wheeler explained, they could not know when they might need to be familiar with the basic layout of Grandview. It was best to take the time to survey their environment now before a crisis could arise.

During the course of their walk, they managed a brief visit with Carlos Mendoza and Juanita Alvarez over in the Mexican portion of town. Over coffee, Carlos related some of his joy at visiting with family and friends from long ago. Obviously, the old man was enjoying the renewal of old family ties, and his niece seemed to take some comfort in the presence of her uncle. Half an hour of small talk passed before Abe and Wheeler set out to continue their exploration of the weathered bordertown.

As the sun rose higher, the day grew warmer. By late morning, the two Bar W cowboys had walked the streets and alleys of the small community enough to be comfortable with their surroundings.

'I believe I could use a cool beer, Mr Davis,' Wheeler grinned at his partner.

'That suits me just fine, Mr McKay.' Abe returned the smile as the two friends strode off in the direction of the only saloon.

Pushing through the batwing doors, Wheeler and Abe paused to let their eyes adjust to the gloomy interior before crossing the sawdust covered floor to the long bar.

'Thanks.' Wheeler nodded his appreciation as he laid a coin upon the bar.

As was his custom, Abe stood with his elbows upon the bar to survey the room. Wheeler got a similar view in the long mirror that hung along the back wall behind the polished mahogany counter.

A few scattered patrons sat at the tables around the barroom, a card game here and a flirtatious bar-girl there, but Abe and Wheeler quickly focused their attention upon the table near the rear wall. At this table sat Big Jake Hollister and Morgan Erskin, Grandview's recently-appointed marshal. The two men were deep in conversation, but managed an occasional glance in the direction of the two new arrivals now standing at the bar. Each pair of men recognised the other and attempted to evaluate the challenge their opponents presented.

'Looks like we're about to meet the big man,' Abe observed as Morgan pushed back his chair to climb to his feet.

'And get our first look at the deadly Morgan Erskin,' added Wheeler as he watched the scene unfold in the mirror.

The frail, slender gunman in the fine grey suit crossed the floor at a careful, casual pace. A bright, bronze star shone from his lapel while the two Smith and Wesson American .44 revolvers hung at his hips. The ivory grips of the pistols gleamed in the dull light of the big saloon. The pale grey eyes and the sharp hook nose gave the man's smile the appearance of a leer as he stopped several feet from the men from Wallaceville. Wheeler slowly, carefully, turned to face the fragile little man.

'Mr Hollister would like to meet you gentlemen if you have the time.' Morgan Erskin's voice was high-pitched, soft, and flat-toned. In spite of his delicate appearance, the small man carried with him an air of danger. His request no more than a thinly veneered command.

'It would be our pleasure,' Wheeler responded with his usual open smile and polite tone. Abe's face grew hard. His eyes narrowed as his hand shifted to be near the grip of the big Remington at his right hip. Morgan only smiled at the giant's angry glare.

They followed the pale gunman back across the room to the table where Big Jake sat in smug silence. Morgan quickly paced around to stand behind the big man's chair and slightly to the right, his arms confidently folded across his chest. Wheeler and Abe came to a halt some few feet from Hollister's table. They stood before the Box H rancher as all present appraised one another. An icy quiet seized the room in a tight fist while the seconds dragged past slowly.

'Have a seat, gentlemen.' Hollister was the first to break silence as he indicated two chairs across the table from him. The man's face beamed a crooked smile that seemed to match the bent nose above the gaping slash of his mouth.

'No thank you,' Wheeler's smile flashed back. 'We'll stand, Mr Hollister.'

There was no question as to how Wheeler knew the big man's identity. Hollister's ego never doubted that he was well known and, he believed, well feared, throughout the state of Texas.

'I understand that Elton Torrence suddenly decided to leave town early this morning.' Hollister came right to the point. His eyes fastened upon Wheeler's face in an effort to intimidate the smaller man.

'Yes,' Wheeler spoke quietly. 'I believe he was lookin' for a healthier place to live.'

'Too bad he never found it.' Hollister's face glowed in triumph as a big fist brought a fat, black cigar to his lips. He puffed blue smoke into the room before continuing. 'Seems the marshal here had to gun down the poor old jasper before he could make it out of town. You know that old Torrence was a notorious shootist. We don't like his kind hangin' around Grandview. A man like that might give this lovely city a bad reputation.'

'You are a tough, sorry old buzzard aren't you, Hollister?' Abe's temper broke and the words burst from a face contorted by anger. Wheeler looked upon the big man seated at the table with cold contempt, but raised a hand to silence his enraged companion.

'Nobody talks to me that way, boy!' Big Jake growled. 'And nobody quits on me. I sent Torrence to do a job. He failed.' The cigar served to bring a pause to the rancher's speech and a cloud of smoke surrounded his head once more. 'And now he's paid the price.'

'So what do you want with us, Hollister?' Wheeler asked, while letting his eyes drift to the smirking gunman standing near the big man's chair. 'Where do we figure into your game here in Grandview?'

'You don't!' Hollister snarled. The town's boss glared across the table at the men standing before him. His eyes blazed hatred that threatened to explode in violence. 'That's just the point. You don't figure into my plans at all. I want you both out of town before sundown. This town ain't got nothin' to offer you boys, and we don't want you hangin' around here. Get on your horses and get the hell outta town before you join Elton Torrence in a shallow grave out back of the trash heap.' Hollister jerked a stubby thumb at the gunman behind him. 'The marshal here don't take kindly to drifters loafing about town. We're strictly a law and order community around these parts.'

'I'm glad to learn that the local law is so concerned about the safety and welfare of the people.' Wheeler mocked the Box H rancher with exaggerated politeness before his tone turned serious. 'We're not leaving town until we see just what's happenin' around here. I want to know what's gone rotten in this town, and,' he added with a hard set to his jaw, 'clean out the trash before I leave.'

'If you know what's good for you then you trouble-makers'll get out of town like I told you!' Hollister roared out the advice, then fell oddly quiet. 'There ain't nothin' nor nobody here 'ceptin' a bunch of damn Mexicans.

What happens to them don't matter to no-body.'

'It matters to us.' Wheeler's reply was definitive. His tone was now cold and hard. Abe nodded his head in agreement with a nasty scowl marking his features.

Hollister let out a whoosh of foul air in a heavy sigh, then rubbed his chin with a dirty paw. His dark eyes met Wheeler's gaze once more before he continued.

'Listen,' the town boss's voice took on a note of reason, 'this is my town. I own more than half the buildings and businesses and my Box H ranch is the only thing that keeps this place alive. People live here and do what I tell 'em. That's the way I like it. If they don't like it, then they can just get the hell outta my town!'

'Unless, of course, they owe you money,' Abe joined the conversation now, 'like all the Mexican people do in these parts.'

'Or,' Wheeler interjected, 'unless they happen to want to leave their jobs like Elton Torrence.'

'You're pretty smart, ain't you boys?' Hollister's eyes narrowed and his voice dropped to a whispered growl. 'Now, you've been warned fair and proper. Get out of town while you're able. Get out of town afore somethin' happens to ruin your day.'

Wheeler and Abe met the rancher's gaze with a cold stare of their own before they turned to angle away from the table. Hollister and Morgan remained in their field of vision as they stepped toward the doorway.

'I know who you are, McKay.' Morgan's voice broke the quiet tension that filled the barroom. The shootist's voice brought the two men up short of the door. 'You beat Elton to the draw and you killed Lance Cardigan up around Wallaceville a while back.'

'That's right,' Wheeler responded without bluster.

'Do like Mr Hollister says, McKay,' Morgan took on a predatory look. 'You might be good but you're not good enough. I'll kill you if it comes to that.'

'Well, now that's kind of you to let me

know,' Wheeler grinned as he offered the gunman a small salute, 'and I'll keep that in mind should the occasion arise.'

Quickly Abe and Wheeler exited the saloon. It seemed to Wheeler that the events were rapidly coming to a head here in Grandview. There was little doubt that hot lead and smoking six guns would be needed before any real peace would be found in this south west Texas bordertown. Wheeler felt the little gunman's eyes upon his back as the men from Wallaceville strode toward the cafe and lunch. There would be a showdown in Grandview for sure.

SEVEN

Instantly, Wheeler came awake and alert in the soft bed in the hotel room he shared with Abe Davis. A slight sound had stirred the Croly County peace officer from his sleep in the pre-dawn darkness. He now lay still under the tattered patchwork quilt listening for some sign of danger. His eyes surveyed the small, standard hotel room; two beds, a washstand with bowl and pitcher, and a couple of ladderback chairs were all the furnishings provided. Everything seemed to be in place. Abe lay across the room in his own bed snoring softly. The noise came again. This time Wheeler recognised the sound.

Keys jingled softly outside the hotel room door; small metallic groans came forth as one of those keys slowly turned the rusty lock. Quickly and silently, Wheeler slipped out of bed to pad across the floor to awaken Abe.

'Company,' was the only word he spoke as he placed a hand on the giant's shoulder while whispering close to his ear.

Without a sound, Abe rose from his bed with the Remington .44 in his fist. Wheeler's Colt .45 already pointed toward the door as the lock clicked. Moments passed as those on the other side waited to see if their movements had been detected.

Abe and Wheeler had spent a leisurely afternoon following their meeting with Hollister and Morgan. Lunch at the cafe had preceded another thorough reconnaissance of the entire community. Early evening had, once again, found them enjoying a big dinner in the tiny *cantina* with Carlos and Juanita. A couple of drinks in the downstairs saloon had brought to a conclusion their uneventful afternoon. Big Jake Hollister's 'sundown' ultimatum had come and gone without incident. The two Bar W cowboys had called it an early night.

Now, they waited with pistols in hand for uninvited guests in the early morning hour before dawn. Both had known the peaceful afternoon could not last. Both understood that Big Jake Hollister would not allow them to remain in town unchallenged.

Satisfied now that the element of surprise would be on their side, the unknown visitors turned the knob of the big oak door. Suddenly the panel flew inward. The light from the hallway broke through the open portal. Two men leaped into the dark room with revolvers in hand. The quiet of the night shattered by gunfire, each man directed his fire into one of the recently vacated beds. Coming from the lighted hallway into the night-black of the hotel room, neither gunman could tell that the beds were now empty. The night raiders placed four shots into the beds, assuming the lead slugs found the sleeping forms of the troublesome strangers they had been sent to eliminate.

'You think they're dead?' one of the squat forms asked in the darkened room. It was one of the killers of Paco Montoya.

'Hell yeah, they're dead!' another man snickered in the night. He too had been with the big man, Luke, when they murdered the protector of Juanita Alvarez.

'Sorry boys, but you're way off target.' Wheeler's voice was soft and quiet.

Both men jerked around in shocked surprise to blaze away with ready pistols even before they could locate targets.

Boom!

Abe's .44 roared into the small room. His shot smacked into the gunman's chest with a sickening thud. A grunt of pain escaped the outlaw's lips as he slumped to the carpet.

Boom!

Wheeler's .45 sounded almost in unison with his companion's revolver. The lead from the Peacemaker punched a black hole through the raider's cheek before exiting the back of his skull. The pudgy man made no sounds as he fell backward to sprawl upon the floor.

Both men were dead when they hit the worn, faded carpet. The two lifeless forms were illuminated by the yellow splash of light that passed through the open doorway. Each figure leaked crimson into pools that seemed to match the floral pattern of the rug.

'How 'bout scare up a candle from the washstand drawer, Abe? Let's see what we got here,' Wheeler requested.

The giant's form moved through the room in compliance. Passing through the long rectangle of light that spilled through the doorway from the lighted hall, Abe was momentarily illuminated. In that brief instant, a shot rang out from the hallway. Lead crackled past the big man's head as he dropped to the floor, rolling for whatever small cover he might find in the sparsely furnished room.

Movement came from the hall along with the sound of boots in rapid retreat down the long, narrow corridor, that led to the stairs. In a flash, Wheeler stepped through the doorway into the light of this passageway.

'Stop!' He shouted the warning immediately before firing a round wide of the fleeing night raider. At the sound of the shot, the big man at the far end of the hall twisted in mid-stride to fire twice in response. His shots passed far from their mark as he pulled the trigger in haste. Wheeler's next shot did not.

Boom!

The Peacemaker sounded again. The big man dropped the revolver to fall against the wall. A growing patch of scarlet soaked into his shirt and pants surrounding the hole just above his belt buckle. Slumping to the floor, he left a crimson streak along the wall as he came to rest in a sitting position, staring at the man who cautiously approached from down the corridor. The dying man was the last of the trio that had murdered Paco; the big one known as Luke.

'Looks like hard livin'' has done caught up with me.' Luke forced a painful lopsided grin while deep scarlet drops escaped his nose and fell from the corners of his mouth.

'I'd say so,' Wheeler stated matter-of-factly as Abe joined him beside the crumpled figure.

'You mind tellin' us who put you up to this?' Abe queried the big man.

'Hell,' Luke coughed a spray of blood that stained his shirt front, 'you know who put us up to it. Only one man runs the show around here in Grandview. You boys are holdin' a losin' hand...' The man's voice faded into a desperate gurgle as he struggled to keep his eyes open.

'Jake Hollister just don't take no for an answer,' Abe observed to no one in particular.

'Somehow,' Luke croaked out a raspy whisper, 'I just never thought it would end up like this.' The man's eyes closed. His head fell forward upon his chest.

'They never do,' Wheeler commented as he replaced the spent shells in the .45. He and Abe returned to their room to dress and await the arrival of Grandview's marshal. They had no doubt that the shots would quickly bring the town's dangerous little lawman.

They did not have long to wait. Within five minutes Marshal Morgan Erskin swaggered into the hotel room. Still dressed in the immaculate grey suit with matching derby, the frail, small man came to a stop some five feet inside the open doorway.

'Did you boys leave that body out there in the hall?' Morgan's lips were set in a sneer. 'You know we got laws against this sort of thing.'

'I'm afraid the intruders left us little choice,' Wheeler responded as he rose from the ladder-back chair upon which he had waited the arrival of the local law. On the other side of the room, Abe came to his feet as well. 'You can see,' Wheeler nodded toward the two beds evidencing the recent bullet holes, 'these gentlemen had murder on their minds.'

As he spoke another man entered the room. The hard rugged face of Chester Alison showed no emotion as he surveyed the carnage upon the floor of the hotel room. He offered the room's occupants only the briefest of glances along with an almost imperceptible nod. A shiny deputy badge had been added to his grey shirt, but otherwise the tall figure looked the same as when the Bar W hands had met him along the trail a few days before.

'Y'all wanna tell me what's happened here?' Morgan spoke sharply as Alison came to stand behind him with his hands on his hips. The hard man's eyes offered no clue to his thoughts.

'We were sleeping when these men decided to enter our room without an invitation,' Wheeler explained as Abe looked on with a hand near his Remington. 'They burst into the room firing shots into our beds. Fortunately for us,' a slight grin played across his handsome features, 'we weren't in them at the time. We exchanged shots and they came up short. There you've got the results.' He indicated the crumpled forms with a wave of his left hand. His right remained close to the walnut grip of the .45.

Morgan briefly shook his head in a gesture that bordered upon professional respect for a job well done. Alison let his eyes move from one figure to the other; his face still remained blank.

'And that feller in the hallway; what about him?' The marshal asked, but his tone indicated disinterest.

'He fired a shot into the room from the doorway, then took off down the hall.' Wheeler told the story briefly. 'I followed after him. He's dead and I'm not. Anything else you need to know?'

'No,' Morgan met Wheeler's hazel eyes. 'I think I've got your story. That don't mean I like it and it don't mean I believe it either. It seems to me that you two fellers ain't been nothin' but trouble ever since you showed up here in our city.'

Wheeler and Abe offered no response. Each kept a steady watch focused upon the fragile gunfighter. Both were ready to pull their pistols if necessary.

'You know,' Morgan began in his soft, deadly voice, 'if you two had left town like Mr Hollister asked, then these three men would still be alive.'

'And if they hadn't tried to kill us in our sleep they'd still be alive too,' Abe interjected.

Morgan's eyes flashed something dangerous and Abe fell silent as he waited to hear what the marshal had to say.

'I could arrest you both on charges of murder,' the lawman stated with grim satisfaction. 'Now, those charges might not stick, but then again,' he paused to offer up a sneer, 'you boys might not be alive when a trial date came up anyway. Lots of things can happen once you get locked up behind bars in a strange town.'

'So, why don't you spell it out, Morgan?' Wheeler's tone was cold. He knew what was coming.

'I'm tellin' you troublemakers for the last time,' the marshal's pale, grey eyes flashed death, 'get out of town now!'

'And if we don't...' Abe never had the

chance to finish his question.

'You will,' Morgan observed. 'You have no choice.' A leering grin animated the gunman's features. 'Earlier this evening I found it necessary to make an arrest over in Mex town. I got an old man and his niece locked up in my jail right now.' He paused, enjoying the stunned looks upon the faces before him. 'If you're not gone within the hour I'll kill the old man, and the girl...' He didn't complete his statement but the sadistic look in his eyes left little doubt regarding his plans for Juanita Alvarez.

'And when we've gone...' Wheeler began the question.

'Why we'll let the worthless old man and his slut of a niece go. We're honourable men, Mr McKay.' Morgan mocked the two ranch hands. 'Besides,' the lawman continued, 'you got no choice in the matter. If you ain't gone within the hour they're both dead. It's as simple as that.'

'What's to prevent me from killin' you on the spot right where you stand?' Abe's level voice broke through the stillness.

'Well, now that's a good question, boy.' Morgan's lips turned up in his predator's grin. 'In the first place, I'd put a bullet through your skull afore you ever touched that pistol of yours.' His eyes burned with confidence as he responded to the challenge. 'In the second place, my men over at the jail house have instructions. If they so much as hear a gunshot, any gunshot, they're gonna kill the old man and that girl.' He paused to meet the brown, hate-filled eyes of Abe Davis. 'You got any other questions, boy?'

Abe shook his head in silence. Wheeler looked on with a hard set to his jaw.

'Now, I'm headin' back over to the law office. My deputy here,' the marshal jerked a thumb at Alison, 'is gonna stick with you boys to make sure you two make it out of town within that hour.' Morgan turned to walk out the door, but hesitated just as he stepped into the hallway. 'Y'all have a nice trip, you hear? And boys,' the pale thin lips turned upwards in a mocking grin, 'don't y'all come back to see us any more.'

Icy silence gripped the room as all present listened to the soft steps of Morgan Erskin retreat down the corridor before descending the stairs. At last Wheeler shifted his gaze to the hard man who stood just inside the door.

'Is this the way it has to be, Alison?' Wheeler asked quietly. There was no challenge in his voice.

'I just work for the man, McKay.'

'That doesn't answer my question.'

'You're damn right it answers your question.' The man's eyes narrowed. His muscles tensed. 'I work for Erskin and the marshal works for Hollister. They say you two are leaving town before the sun comes up, and it's my job to see that you do it. Like Morgan said,' the deputy shook his head slightly, 'there really ain't no choice in the matter.'

'You reckon this is the right thing to do?' Abe asked the question only to be silenced by a withering glare from the flat expressionless face of the deputy.

'Don't give me no Sunday school lesson,' Alison snarled, and for the first time a fleeting look of anger passed over his features. 'I'm a gunman past my prime and lookin' for steady work. Mayor Hollister and Marshal Erskin say I've got a future with the Box H organisation. This deputy job here in Grandview is made to order for me, and I don't aim to let it slip through my fingers just to save some damn old Mexican and his niece.' He took a deep breath then barked out a command. 'Now pack up your saddle bags and get the hell out of town while you still can.'

'You live with it, Alison.' Wheeler turned to pick up his saddle bags and began stuffing his belongings into the leather pouches. Abe did the same.

The bright orange globe hung high in the blue Texas sky, warming the two riders and taking the chill off the fall day. It was just past noon. Abe and Wheeler had been on the trail since before sunrise, Grandview now several hours behind them along the long, dusty path.

'He still back there?' Abe brought the big bay close alongside Jim, Wheeler's big black stallion. 'I ain't seen nothin' of 'im for more than an hour now.'

'I think he's turned back,' Wheeler observed. 'Soon as we head down the other side of this rise here we'll pull up and watch our back trail.'

Coming down the other side of the rocky incline, Wheeler brought Jim to a halt as Abe did the same to his own mount. The two men climbed down from the saddle to scurry back to the top of the hill and lie patiently on their bellies for the next half hour. Each man let his eyes carefully survey the horizon stretched out before them. Barren, rocky land of south west Texas lay bleak and deserted. Except for the occasional lizard or insect, Wheeler and Abe saw no sign of life as they watched the landscape for the man who had followed them at a distance since leaving Grandview.

'He'd have shown up by now if he was still

on our tail,' Abe observed in a whisper.

'No doubt about it!' Wheeler announced as he rose to his feet to clamber down the embankment in the direction of Jim. The big charcoal waited patiently for his master, nickering softly at Wheeler's arrival.

All morning the men had been aware of the furtive activity along their back trail. The man had been good, but not good enough to go undetected. Obviously, Big Jake Hollister had wanted to make certain that the two men did not simply double back to Grandview as soon as they were clear of the town limits. Satisfied that the strangers were well on their way back to Wallaceville, the man who had trailed them had, at last, returned to report to his employer.

Reaching Jim, Wheeler poured water from his canteen into the faded grey Confederate hat he now held in his left palm. Jim stuffed his nose down in the hat to lap greedily at the tepid water as the Croly County lawman scratched between the animal's twitching ears.

'We'll rest the horses for about an hour,' Wheeler looked on as Abe watered his own mount. 'I could use a little nap myself.' He grinned at the giant. 'It seems my sleep was rudely interrupted last night.'

'That ought to put us back in Grandview some time after dark.' Abe flashed his companion an enthusiastic smile.

'Big Jake's grown a bit too sure of himself,' Wheeler answered back with a grim smile of his own. 'The mayor and the marshal might order us out of town, but if they wanted us to keep out of Grandview then they should've had their rider follow us all the way back to Wallaceville.'

'If they wanted to keep me out of Grandview,' Abe sobered and his brown eyes took on a determined look, 'they should've killed me while they had the chance.'

Nothing more was said. The two loosened the saddle cinches before stretching out upon the hard earth for a few moments of rest. Night would bring a violent climax to the events of the past few days. Darkness would bring death and a conclusion to the struggle between justice and oppression in the small Texas bordertown.

EIGHT

In the full darkness of late evening, Abe and Wheeler made their way cautiously down the cluttered alley that ran alongside the combination jail house and marshal's office. Halting briefly to crouch behind a massive pile of refuse, the two had begun a whispered conversation.

'What's the plan?' Abe asked with concern bringing an edge to his soft rumble.

'I kind of hoped you had one,' Wheeler responded with a wry grin that became lost in the black of night. His attempt at humour brought only a heavy sigh from the giant at his side.

'We'd better think of something,' Abe growled urgently.

'And fast,' came his partner's reply.

All humour seemed to have quickly

evaporated in the cool fall evening that held Grandview in a tight fist.

The two Bar W ranch hands had spent the entire afternoon returning to the troubled bordertown. Arriving on the outskirts of town just after sunset, Wheeler and Abe had shared a meal of canned peaches and water before securing their horses in a small stand of scrub trees and brush just north and east of the town limits. Both men were now thankful for the hours spent the day before in exploring the town's streets and alleys, for they were able to make their way to the marshal's office undetected using back streets and alleyways. Now, having surveyed the jail house from the back and sides, they sat, slumped against an outside wall, puzzled by their next move. Everything hinged on their ability to free Carlos and Juanita.

'From what I could see through the windows,' Abe observed in a quiet voice, 'there's four of 'em in there in the office space up front.'

'Best I could tell, you're right,' Wheeler

confirmed. 'Four hardcases in the front office and our friends locked up in the cell block out back.'

'Well we can't just walk up to the front door and...' Abe stopped short in mid-sentence as a match flared some few feet toward the rear of the building. The tiny flame briefly illuminated the features of the hard man as he puffed a thin, black cigar to life. The glowing stick fell to the earth to be crushed out by the toe of a scuffed boot. The red eye of burning tobacco hung suspended in the dark passageway between the buildings. Wheeler and Abe tensed in anxious expectation of the deputy's next action.

'I figgered you boys'd be back some time tonight,' Alison spoke quietly as calloused fingers withdrew the cigar from between his lips. 'I been waitin' on you.' His left hand returned the tobacco to his mouth. His right hung close to the grip of the short-barrelled Colt .45.

The silence weighed heavy for several

seconds as Wheeler and Abe considered the situation. The lives of Carlos and Juanita rested in their hands. The future of justice in Grandview depended on this evening's showdown with Hollister. Now, just short of their goal, the very man who had ushered them out of town before dawn faced them in a darkened alley outside the marshal's office. Abe's fingers carefully inched toward the grip of his Remington. Wheeler remained silent and still as he regarded the Grandview deputy who had surprised them in the darkness.

'You got a plan?' Alison broke the silence after taking another long draw off the cigar. He exhaled then flipped the glowing stub into the night.

'We were just talkin' about that.' Wheeler's face managed a satisfied smile as the tension drained from his body.

'I might be able to help,' the hard man offered.

'What do you want, Alison?' Abe's voice had a hard edge of suspicion. The giant obviously recalled their early-morning con-frontation with bitterness. 'If you wanted to help then why didn't you do somethin' this mornin' when you were busy runnin' us out of town?'

Chester Alison managed a small grin before replying. 'There weren't nothin' I could do for you boys this mornin'. We was bein' watched real close. Anything we done might well have cost that old man and girl their lives. It was best to play along with the plan. Howsomever, things is settled down now that Hollister and Erskin think you all are gone for good. I can be of help in gettin' them folks out of that jail house.'

'How do we know we can trust you?' Abe questioned the gunman in a harsh whisper.

'You don't,' Alison responded. 'No matter what you might think, I ain't no animal. I live by my gun and my wits, but that don't make me no murderer or thief. I never took nothin' from nobody that I didn't earn. This set-up here stinks of murderers and thieves. I aim to help you fellers clean up afore you pull out of town.' The hard man paused for a moment to let the Bar W cowboys think it all through. 'Now, that's the way it lays, boys. You want my help or not? Let's get this settled so's we can get on with the business at hand.'

'We can use the help,' Abe spoke now with calm assurance. 'Thanks, Alison.'

'The problem is gettin' inside to get Carlos and Juanita out,' Wheeler explained. 'Once they're safe, then we can force a showdown with Hollister and Morgan.'

'Then I suppose we'd best get on with it,' Alison commented dryly.

'Just what have you got in mind, Deputy?' Wheeler asked with a wide grin animating his features.

'Well,' Alison explained, 'I believe the place to start is for you boys to hand over them guns.' As if by magic, the hard man's Colt .45 appeared in his fist. The revolver pointed at the two men from Wallaceville who now struggled to their feet. 'Shuck them irons from the holsters and we'll be on our way.'

'When did Morgan say we could have some fun with that little Mexican gal back there?' Ernie Juzzak twisted his features with a foolish grin. Plump, grey, balding, and unshaved, the man maintained his post seated just outside the barred door leading to the cell block in the rear of the jail house. Dressed in soiled, patched range clothing, Juzzak rubbed at his eyes with dirty paws in an effort to keep himself awake. A Smith and Wesson .44-.40 rested in a battered holster upon his right hip. 'I need a little excitement to keep from fallin' asleep.'

Two men were already stretched out sleeping upon the sagging bunks on opposite sides of the room. The lanky forms of Bill Simmons and Arnie Tredwell were covered by blankets that smelled almost as badly as their unwashed bodies.

A typical small town law office, the littered room contained a battered oak desk, a rack of rifles, a few scattered ladder-backed chairs, and the worn bunks where Simmons and Tredwell snored softly. Trash and refuse spilled from the waste basket to spread throughout the room. Everything seemed covered by grime and filth. Obviously, the law in Grandview had little respect for cleanliness.

'You'd better hold onto your horses, Ernie,' Dexter Hupkanz responded to his old saddle partner in an irritated tone of voice, 'you don't want to rile that Morgan Erskin. The marshal's a mean 'un fer sure.' Hupkanz stood a few inches over five feet and, in contrast to his slovenly old friend, boasted a slender, well-built frame. Neatly combed orange-red hair and a well-trimmed beard marked pleasant features while his range clothes remained in immaculate condition. The clean, neat mask that Dexter Hupkanz habitually wore fronted the mind of a sadistic killer. His pleasant smile and scrubbed good looks had opened many doors to the little man with the old Starr .44 revolver. At the age of thirty, the mild-mannered hardcase had killed seventeen men. 'We'll get our turn with that cute darlin' when Morgan gets back here late tonight. Meanwhile, we'd best keep watch like we been told. I don't want no trouble on this job, Ernie.'

'Hell, I've 'bout had enough of this two-bit...' Juzzak's words were interrupted by a pounding upon the heavy front door.

'Open up there, boys!' Chester Alison's voice sounded from the other side of the thick, oak panel. 'I got prisoners out here.'

Ernie Juzzak never left his chair, but Dexter Hupkanz immediately jumped to his feet to hurry over to the front door of the marshal's office. The two men in the bunks tossed a bit and cursed their partners for some quiet so they could sleep off an afternoon of bad whisky.

'You gonna open the damn door or am I supposed to keep these men out here all night at gun-point?' Alison's tone was impatient and hostile.

'I'm gettin' it, Deputy, I'm gettin' it,' Hupkanz called out as he turned the big brass key in the massive door lock and shot back the iron bolt that held the door in place. He stepped back a few paces from the door to shout, 'It's open!'

'And about time at that,' Alison growled from the outside as Abe and Wheeler pushed through the law office front door.

Hupkanz and Juzzak were startled to see the two troublesome strangers march into the cluttered office space. The Grandview Deputy had his own .45 in his right hand and Wheeler's Peacemaker in his left. Abe's Remington was stuffed in the waist band of his pants. A look of grim determination seemed carved into the hard man's features.

'I found these two varmints hangin' around in the alley,' Alison explained to the astonished men. 'Figgered we better lock 'em up and get word to Marshal Erskin right away.'

'Jehosaphat!' Juzzak exclaimed as he scrambled to his feet. He turned his back to the room while his pudgy fingers fumbled with the massive bolts that secured the cell block door.

Meanwhile, Hupkanz strode across the room to retrieve his neatly creased Stetson from a peg behind the law office desk. For a moment, the immaculate little man faced the wall as he carefully removed his head gear from the rack and gently tugged the hat into place.

'By damn, Morgan'll sure be surprised at this one. Why, Mr Hollister might just give you a bonus, Chester. You know, I'll bet that...' Hupkanz turned to find a Remington Over-and-Under .41 a few feet from his face. Wheeler held the powerful little derringer while his partner, Abe, fisted a similar weapon directly at the portly Juzzak. Alison's two pistols now lined upon the reclining figures in the old rumpled bunks.

'Time to get up, boys,' Alison's voice carried no hint of compromise as the sleepy-eyed hardcases raised their heads to look in the hard man's direction. 'I'd just as soon kill you as look at you so I'll leave it up to you.'

Within four minutes the four Hollister gunmen were tightly bound, hand and foot, gagged, and left upon the dirty floor of a cell in the rear of the jail house. Alison's plan had worked exactly as they had hoped. Carlos Mendoza and Juanita Alvarez had been freed without a single shot being fired. Hollister and Erskin would have no warning of the coming showdown. Now, the old man and his niece sat in the front office with their rescuers; momentarily they allowed their gratitude to overwhelm them.

'*Gracias, mi amigos*,' Carlos enthused for the tenth time since Wheeler had unlocked the iron door of the dark cell out back. 'We were told you had left us, but I knew that you would be back. I knew you would not desert us.'

'*Si*,' Juanita interjected. 'My uncle assured me that all would be well. He never truly believed that you would leave us to Hollister and the men of the Box H ranch.'

'I don't mean to interrupt,' Alison's tone carried a note of cynicism, 'but we'd best get the hell out of here afore Morgan or some of them Box H boys show up and spoil our happy reunion.'

'I expect you're right,' Wheeler grinned at the hard man's gloomy countenance.

'What now?' Abe asked.

'You know where the mayor and the marshal might be at this time of night?' Wheeler directed his question to the deputy.

'Sure,' Alison remarked, 'Hollister and Morgan are both over to the saloon. They'll hang around there till about midnight or so, then Big Jake'll head for his big house here in town and Morgan'll come back to the office to check in on the prisoners.'

'Then,' Wheeler turned to Abe, 'our next move is to pay our respects to Mayor Hollister and Marshal Erskin at the saloon.'

'What about her?' Abe jerked a thumb in the direction of the young girl. 'Does she go with us?'

'Hell, no!' Alison barked out a response without thinking. 'We got 'em loose, now send the old man and the little lady home.

We can't be watchin' out for them when we face down Big Jake and that snake of a marshal.'

'I'm afraid they'll have to stick close by us,' Wheeler held up a hand to silence Alison's objections. 'We really ain't got much choice. We might need to make a quick getaway and we'll need them close by just in case. If we left them here in Grandview we'd just be right back where we started off the night.'

'All right,' growled the deputy, impatient now to be on his way, 'just keep 'em out of my way once the lead starts flyin' inside the saloon.'

Carlos quickly crossed the room to pull his old shotgun down from the rack where Ernie had placed it earlier in the evening. He checked the loads and found his canvas pouch of spares in a nearby desk drawer.

'What about it, Carlos?' Wheeler met the elder's level stare. 'Can we count on you to watch after Juanita and keep clear of the action?'

'Si, Senor McKay,' the old man solemnly

shook his head, 'I am but a frail and feeble servant in my declining years. I only patiently await my time to die. Surely, I could have nothing to contribute to this grand battle you are about to undertake.'

Alison scowled. Wheeler looked doubtful. Abe grinned while offering Carlos a wink of friendly support.

Chester Alison stepped through the rear door of the jail house to make certain the small group of allies could exit unobserved. They made their way through back streets until reaching the livery stable. At the big barn, Alison used his position as deputy marshal to commandeer five sturdy horses for the group before they proceeded on to the alley that bordered the rear of the big saloon and hotel. After a brief, whispered conversation, Carlos and Juanita were left with the horses to keep the animals ready in case the need arose for a hasty retreat. Carlos smiled broadly at the assignment.

'Have no fears, brave *hombres,*' the old man voiced in a hoarse whisper, 'your humble servant awaits your triumphant return.' Abe snickered softly at the sarcasm and even Wheeler could not repress a smile. Carlos would be hard to live with by the time they got him back to the Circle D.

'He's beginnin' to get on my nerves,' Alison grumbled as the three men stepped to the back door and the deputy turned the knob slowly. 'I'll go first. If anybody's back here in the storeroom I might be able to stall off questions long enough to take care of 'em for good.'

The deputy cautiously opened the door then pushed through into the dimly lit store-room. The short-barrelled Colt gripped tightly in his fist, Alison surveyed the narrow room with stacks of crates piled almost to the ceiling. Two steps inside the door, he heard a voice call out from behind a stack of boxes.

'Who in blazes is that?' It was the scrawny little bartender with the gaunt face and shrivelled features. He poked his head around the corner with a nasty look contorting his weasel-face and a Smith and Wesson Pocket .38 in his left fist. 'Oh,' he grinned in relief as he stuffed the pistol into his waist band, 'it's you Deputy. I heard the door open and didn't know…'

The barkeep stopped talking as he caught sight of Wheeler and Abe stepping through the open doorway behind the deputy lawman. Clawing for his revolver with bony fingers, the drink dispenser opened his mouth for a warning scream. He was too slow.

Alison closed the gap between them to swing his pistol in a swift arc that ended atop the greasy head of the shrivelled saloon keeper. A sigh escaped the little man's withered lips as his eyes crossed before he fell to the floor in a rumpled heap. For good measure, the hard man stuffed the man's soiled bandana in his mouth for a temporary gag and used the limp figure's belt to bind the claw-like hands behind his back.

'That ought to hold 'im while we take care of matters out front,' Alison commented as he rose to his feet. 'How's it look out there?'

'Could be worse,' Wheeler observed without humour. His soft voice was matter-of-fact, evidencing no sign of fear. 'I can see Hollister over at his usual table along with Morgan. I can't see the whole room from here, but I'd guess there's another five or six Box H hands scattered about the barroom.'

'We got our work cut out for us tonight.' Abe voiced the concern shared by the trio of men now hidden in the saloon's rear store-room.

'It ain't gonna get any easier standing back here thinkin' about it,' Alison growled, his usual impatience heightened by the stress of the coming showdown. 'Let's get on with it.'

'And get it over with,' Abe added.

'So, we shall, gentlemen.' Wheeler offered up a confident smile as he gently pushed open the storeroom door and boldly stepped into the large barroom. Abe and Alison followed close behind. Each man carried a pistol in his hand ready for action.

'I hate to interrupt your fun,' Wheeler's

voice carried above the noisy buzz of conversation and laughter, 'but the party is over here in Grandview.'

NINE

Silence gripped the room as all eyes shifted to the trio of gunmen entering through the rear door of the saloon. Wheeler had been close to the mark with his estimate of the Box H strength present in the barroom. Six hardcase gunnies were scattered about the open space. Each packed at least one revolver strapped about his hips; some carried an extra weapon either openly or concealed. Waiting fingers hovered near pistol grips. All stood poised, tensed, and waiting, in anticipation of the coming showdown.

Wheeler advanced some ten feet into the room while Abe and Alison moved forward to flank him on either side. The Croly County peace officer focused his attention upon Big Jake Hollister and his hired marshal, the fragile Morgan Erskin. Alison and Abe kept a careful watch over the remaining Box H owlhoots. The entire situation was a powderkeg in search of a flaming match.

'Well, well, well,' a big grin broke out over Hollister's blocky, square-jawed features, 'it appears I've underestimated you, Mr McKay.' The smile faded into a determined scowl. 'I won't make that mistake again.'

'You've underestimated Texas justice, Hollister,' Wheeler's tone remained level but firm. 'You're through here in Grandview. It can be easy or hard, but the time has come for you, Morgan, and the rest of your Box H scum to move along; leave these people in peace.'

'Don't talk to me about, "justice",' Hollister growled. 'You might be a big dog up around Wallaceville but you've got no jurisdiction around here. I'm the law in these parts, McKay. Besides,' a confident grin returned to the rugged features of Grandview's mayor, 'that's big talk for a man facin'' these odds; we outnumber you more than two to one. Not to mention my ace-in-the-hole over to the jail house. Now, we wouldn't want anything to happen to that nice old man and his...'

'Save it!' Abe interrupted the big man seated across the room. 'We've already taken care of your hostages from the jail cell. We're here to finish our business with you and the marshal.'

The smile rapidly faded from Hollister's face. The news momentarily shook the rancher's confidence. Morgan Erskin quickly joined the heated conversation to cover for his boss.

'Where do you fit into all this, Alison?' Morgan's soft, high-pitched voice sounded almost delicate in the quiet room. 'I thought you were on the right side of things in Grandview.'

'I am,' the hard man answered without emotion. 'I'm here to clean out the trash.' He pulled the badge from his shirt to drop it into the sawdust at his feet.

'That's a big mistake, Alison.' The marshal's eyes blazed deadly hatred even though his voice never changed expression.

'I don't think so.' The hard man's confident tone sounded cold in the tense atmosphere of the saloon stand-off.

'I should've had you killed when I had the chance.' Hollister's voice broke into the conversation now. His tone cold, hard, and bitter.

'You tried hard enough,' Wheeler grinned in spite of the danger that filled the air. 'It'll take a better man than you, Hollister. You're just a small-time outlaw with big ideas. You've played out a lucky string but your luck's come to an end. Pack up and move along. It's the only chance I'll give you.'

'Damn you, McKay!' the Box H boss roared. 'I'll kill you if it's the last thing I ever do!'

With a growl from deep in his chest, Big Jake tipped over the heavy oak table before him. With great speed for a man of his size and bulk, Hollister dropped from sight behind the large wooden slab. In a flash, he was joined in hiding by the pale gunman, Morgan Erskin.

Wheeler snapped off a shot that punched a hole through the oak surface of the bar table, but could not focus his attention on the two men hidden there. As soon as Hollister made his move, gunfire erupted throughout the saloon. The six hardcase Box H cowboys went into action in a concerted effort to bring down the trio facing them across the sawdust covered floor.

Even as Wheeler's Peacemaker boomed in the big room, Abe and Alison had already found targets among the men who hastened to pull iron and enter the shootout. Two shots from Alison punched holes in the squat figure of a rugged gunhawk near the front doors while Abe's Remington accounted for a lanky owlhoot standing at the bar. Both stirred sawdust as they collapsed upon the plank floor into growing pools of crimson. The roar of gunfire filled the barroom; the acrid gunsmoke stung the eyes and noses of all present.

Wheeler turned his attention to a tall, solid-built man levelling twin Colt Frontier .45 revolvers in his direction. His own Peacemaker boomed once. The leering face of the two-gun adversary disappeared in an explosion of scarlet. Before the body hit the floor, the Croly County sheriff had shifted his stance to fire once more at yet another figure whose weapon roared in unison with his own.

Chester Alison felt the lead smack heavily into his left shoulder. The impact of the slug yanked him into a half turn as yet another bullet ripped a ragged hole through his left calf. Numbing shock preceded an over-whelming wave of pain as the hard man, off-balance, fell to the sawdust floor still gripping his short-barrelled .45 tightly in his fist.

Meanwhile, Wheeler's Colt boomed twice bringing down the man who had placed the bullet in Alison's shoulder. Abe's Remington dispatched the owlhoot who had shot the hard man in the leg. One gunman managed a desperate scream of pain and despair as he fell to the floor. Both men were dead within moments of the gun battle's opening shots.

Two tremendous blasts from just inside the back door took everyone by surprise. The final Box H gunman seemed to explode against a wall; virtually cut in two. Blood and gore splattered the surface behind the hardcase as the scarlet mass fell heavily to the floor in a dead, ruined heap.

For a brief moment, Wheeler and Abe shifted their attention to the slender figure who stood near the storeroom door. Carlos Mendoza had saved Wheeler's life. The last of the gunhawks had been set to fire upon the Bar W rancher when the old man had triggered both barrels of his sawed-off American Arms 12-gauge shotgun. The results had been devastating. The lead balls had mangled the man's torso beyond recognition. For his old Wallaceville companions, Carlos offered a grim smile and a small salute.

The six Box H gun hands were dead.

Considering those previously killed and the four men locked away at the jail house, the battle for Grandview seemed firmly in the hands of the men from Croly County. With only one man down, the Bar W hands could count themselves fortunate indeed.

Alison groaned as he struggled to sit up. Blood produced an ever-widening stain about his left shoulder while the nasty hole in his left leg also flowed a stream of scarlet into a small puddle upon the floor. Attempting to use an elbow for leverage, the hard man collapsed into the sawdust with a low moan of pain.

Without hesitation, Wheeler and Abe moved toward the fallen deputy as Carlos began crossing the floor in the same direction. Almost immediately, Wheeler recognised his mistake and began to swing about with the Peacemaker moving toward the overturned table where Hollister and Morgan had waited throughout the gun battle; hoping for some opportunity at escape or revenge.

'Too late, McKay!' Morgan's whining voice challenged the lawman from Wallaceville. Wheeler stopped short as he viewed the scene before him. Apparently, Juanita had grown concerned over the welfare of her uncle and had followed the old man into the saloon. Seeing his opportunity to seize a measure of victory from the ragged edge of defeat, the pale shootist had grabbed the girl from behind as she entered the barroom from the rear door.

'Drop the guns, boys. The shootin' is all over for you folks.' Morgan stood with an arm locked about the throat of Juanita while one of his ornate Smith and Wesson American .44 revolvers pressed firmly against her temple. 'I mean drop 'em now!'

Without another thought, Wheeler and Abe let the pistols fall to the floor. Carlos met the marshal's gaze before tossing the big shotgun into a pile of scarlet sawdust near the body of the man he had recently blasted with the fearsome weapon. All stood by with eyes fixed upon the Grandview lawman who held the frightened young girl captive.

'Can we tend to Alison here?' Abe indicated the bloody form of the deputy now lying sprawled upon the floor. 'He looks to be hurt pretty bad.'

'You stay right where you are, boy!' The hulking frame of Big Jake Hollister lightly rose to his feet from behind the oak table. 'You're all gonna die anyway so you might as well let him bleed to death right where he lies. That's all the two-timing jasper deserves anyhow.'

Alison did not stir again. Apparently the man had mercifully drifted into unconsciousness. Abe hoped that the end would come without pain for the man who had risked his life to help them. The giant held his ground as he kept his attention upon the frail gunman who gripped the Alvarez girl as his hostage.

'You see, boys,' Morgan chuckled as he began his explanation of events, 'you all just ain't got these here women figgered out.

That's what your problem is.' Wheeler, Abe, and Carlos listened helplessly as the little gunman continued. 'I knew this here female couldn't help but come a runnin' when she heard all this commotion in here, so I just waited quietly for the chance to grab her when she stuck her curious little nose into the room. It was just a matter of time.' The marshal chuckled with the sound of rattling bones.

'Now,' Hollister's face seemed to split wide in an enormous smile that showed off yellowed teeth to the men around him, 'you bastards have caused me a lot of trouble the last couple of days and I aim to kill you all.' He cracked the knuckles of his big, scarred fists before continuing. 'First, I'm gonna take this young pup apart with my bare hands.' He jabbed a fat finger at Wheeler as he began to remove his coat.

'Morgan!' Hollister bellowed after draping the coat over an empty chair.

'Yes, sir, Mr Hollister.'

'You watch them other two while I give

this jasper the beatin' he deserves.' Stubby fingers rolled up his sleeves; Hollister's eyes sparkled with anticipation as they fixed upon the rancher from Croly County.

'I'll keep 'em out of your way, Mr Hollister.' Morgan thumbed back the hammer on the .44. His eyes twinkled with sadistic pleasure. 'You gents stay real calm and still now. It'd be a shame if anything was to happen to this pretty young lady.'

Abe and Carlos stood by in motionless silence as they let their own eyes move back and forth from the pale gunman and his trembling captive to the hulking form of Big Jake Hollister who had now crossed the floor to stand before Wheeler McKay.

'You should've stayed home where you belonged, McKay.' Hollister glared at the powerful man who met his hard gaze without flinching.

'Somebody had to bring justice to Grandview.'

'Looks like it won't be you,' Hollister smirked. 'This ain't none of your business anyway, boy.'

'Hollister,' Wheeler shook his head slowly, 'your kind will never understand. This is 1890. I'm a Texas peace officer. Scum like you are like a cancer. If you're not stopped then you eat at all that's good and decent in this state. Before long, Texas wouldn't be a fit place for a family like mine. Injustice is my business, Hollister, whether it's in Croly County or a small bordertown like Grandview. Now,' Wheeler offered the big man a grim smile, 'are we gonna fight or we gonna talk this thing to death?'

'Buster,' Big Jake roared out a challenge at the smaller man standing just a few feet before him, 'you'll beg me to kill you before I'm finished.'

Wheeler never hesitated. Without another word, the Croly County lawman stepped forward to smash a hard right fist into the big man's mouth. He followed this with a solid left-right combination to the man's over-sized belly. A whoosh of foul breath escaped Hollister's lips while blood trickled down his chin. Big Jake spit a yellowed tooth to the sawdust floor as he brought a swift left hook to pound Wheeler's right ear. The punch sent the young man staggering back several paces. The brawling town boss leaped upon him with flashing speed. A punishing left jab opened up Wheeler's right cheek, followed by a right hook that shook the lawman's head. Hollister laughed now in spite of the blood that dripped from his own chin to stain the front of the starched white shirt.

'Come on, son,' the big man roared his amusement. 'You've got to do better than this. Give me a little fight now.'

Wheeler felt warm blood flow from the open wound upon his cheek. He caught his breath and waited in silence for the larger man to approach. He did not have long to wait.

Hollister stepped in quickly behind a stiff left jab. Wheeler darted his head to one side as the punch slipped past his ear. Ducking the right hook he knew would follow, the

Bar W rancher smashed a left to the ribs that brought an audible grunt from Big Jake. An uppercut to the blocky chin jerked the man's head back with a snap. In response, the Grandview mayor launched a wild right that missed Wheeler's head as he bobbed and weaved before the bulky giant. Another left to Hollister's ribs, a right to the mid-section, two jabs to the nose, and a powerful right hook that split open the big man's right ear were all delivered in a whirlwind of punches that overwhelmed the towering town boss.

Wheeler's hands ached. He struggled for breath. Thinking his opponent must be out on his feet, the Bar W rancher stepped back a few paces anticipating the fall of the huge Box H cattle king.

Jake Hollister was a mess. Blood seeped from his battered mouth and nose while crimson flowed freely from his right ear. The giant wobbled for a moment, swayed a bit to his left, then his knees seemed to buckle. Instead of falling forward, the veteran brawler swiftly stepped toward his opponent to unleash a round-house right that caught Wheeler on the side of his head. The blow sent the lawman to the floor after knocking him back and over a small, pine table that stood in his pathway.

An enraged roar escaped Big Jake's lips as he stalked forward smashing the table with big, deadly fists. The little pine plank splintered into fragments as Hollister advanced upon the prone form of his adversary. His face a bloody mask of hatred, the big man's every instinct drove him forward to finish his wounded adversary.

Wheeler sat up shaking his head to clear the ringing sensation that clouded his thinking. He looked up in time to see a boot swing toward his head and managed to move quickly enough to minimise the impact. Still, the blow sent him back to the sawdust. He rolled to his left to avoid the heel of Hollister's right boot that stomped down at his head. Immediately, he kicked out and connected with the giant's knee. Big

Jake gasped in pain as he hobbled back a step to rub at the throbbing agony with a massive paw.

Taking advantage of the break in the action, Wheeler scrambled to his feet. Both were now much the worse for wear. Neither was ready to give it up.

Feinting with a left, Wheeler advanced upon the big man to unload a powerful straight right hand that ruined what remained of the shapeless mass Hollister had called a nose. Crimson spurted from the busted lump soaking the already stained shirt front and leaking heavy drops upon the floor. Momentarily stunned by the sharp pain from his broken nose, Big Jake was not prepared for the right-left combinations that rocked his head from side to side. In desperation, the Grandview boss swung his powerful fists in wild, looping punches that failed to connect.

Wheeler stepped in close to slam a vicious left to his opponent's ribs that brought a satisfying pop. Another left brought a second resounding crack accompanied by a sharp cry of anguished pain from Jake Hollister. The Box H rancher now stumbled backwards with his hands stretched out before him. The bloody paws waved away the powerful young man as the hulking behemoth staggered through the sawdust with loud, agonised groans.

'Stop,' he moaned through lips smashed and bloody, 'stop it, McKay. I'm done in; my insides is busted up.'

Hollister backed up to the long, mahogany bar where he let his elbows support his weight. His big, muscled frame sagged heavily. The blocky, square-jawed features were now a bloody mask. The big man scowled across the floor at the scarlet stained victor of the epic fistic struggle.

'Ain't no man ever beat me with his fists, McKay,' Hollister grumbled in a low growl of frustration, 'and you ain't either.' With that warning, Big Jake snatched a brown whiskey bottle from the scarred counter top and smashed the glass container against the hard wood with a crash. Broken glass tinkled across the scratched surface. Hollister now stood holding the jagged remains of the shattered bottle in his right fist. With a sadistic, leering grin and a glazed stare, the Box H rancher advanced upon the Croly County sheriff once again.

'I'm gonna gut you with this glass, boy!' Big Jake shouted a triumphant roar. 'I'm gonna cut open your belly and leave you to die right here on the barroom floor.'

Wheeler sighed and shook his head in determined resignation. He knew now how the fight would end. Without a doubt, he knew how it would have to end.

Drawing the Bowie from the beaded sheath at his left hip, he quickly stepped inside the range of the approaching giant. Dodging the sharp edges of the broken bottle, Wheeler's razor sharp Bowie slashed rapidly and deeply at the big man's mid-section. The Wallaceville peace officer stepped back a pace now to watch the look of astonishment pass over the rancher's face.

Hollister's shirt front gaped open across the belly where scarlet now flowed from the deep cut that ran side to side. An enraged bellow sounded from the man's open, bloody mouth as he staggered forward toward the swift young man with the Bowie. Thrusting the broken bottle before him in a clumsy gesture, the Grandview mayor attacked once again. It was the last act of a desperate man.

The big blade sank deep in Jake Hollister's chest as Wheeler side-stepped the slashing whiskey bottle. Wallaceville's sheriff paced back. As he did so, Wheeler tugged the Bowie loose. The hole in Hollister's chest squirted crimson across the floor. A puzzled look upon his face, Big Jake crashed to the floor. A brightly polished boot kicked up sawdust, then the big man lay still.

Holding the bloody blade at his side, Wheeler returned his attention to Morgan Erskin. The frail, grey gunman held the young woman in a tight grip with his .44 pressed firmly against her temple.

'You'd better drop that Bowie, McKay,' Morgan grinned his predator's smile. 'This time the party is really over.'

TEN

Wheeler dropped the crimson stained Bowie into the sawdust at his feet. Battered and weary, the Bar W rancher faced the pale, grey little man with the big Smith and Wesson .44 revolvers. The sheriff from Croly County seemed relaxed. His hard hazel eyes carried an air of confidence oddly out of place in the midst of this atmosphere of impending death and destruction.

'Looks like you're callin' the shots.' The calm of Wheeler's voice contrasted with the growing mood of tension in the room. 'What now, Morgan?'

Abe and Carlos looked on in angry silence while the Grandview marshal continued his tight grip upon the captive girl. The sadistic killer with a badge seemed to enjoy the anxious stares sent his direction by the giant

191

black man and his elderly Mexican companion.

'Hell,' Morgan smirked, 'anybody can figure that out, McKay.'

With that said, the gunfighter released his hold upon Juanita Alvarez to propel her toward her uncle with a hard shove of his hand. The beautiful young woman stumbled as she ran into the waiting arms of the slender old man. As all eyes briefly turned to the girl, Morgan quickly drew the matching .44 from his left-hand holster. Both pistols out and levelled the leering gunman seemed in complete command of the saloon-turned-battleground. Obviously, Morgan Erskin enjoyed being in command.

'Any fool'd know that I got to kill you folks,' the marshal stated with a matter-of-fact assurance. 'Like you said, McKay, the game's up here in Grandview. You've brought an end to Hollister's hold on this little town. I'll have to move on.' The predator's smile flashed across his features once more. 'But I'm damned if I won't leave your dead bodies behind afore I go.'

'What's the point of it…' Wheeler tried to stall the frail man with conversation. He hoped to buy time for a possible break toward freedom for his friends.

'I don't have to explain myself to you,' Morgan cut the young man short. 'I'll kill you 'cause I want to or any other reason that suits me. I'll kill you 'cause you ruined a good deal for me here in Grandview and,' he met Wheeler's hazel eyes with a hate-filled stare, 'cause I don't want to leave no witnesses behind when I'm gone. Hell. I'll kill you just for my pleasure.'

'You know,' Wheeler's conversational tone grated upon the gunfighter's nerves, 'I don't think you're man enough to do the job.' The words were designed to stir the gunman's emotions. Wheeler hoped to goad the killer into some action that would provide an opportunity for escape or retaliation. Seemingly, the words had little effect upon the small man with the big .44 pistols. He stood patiently across the saloon from the

Wallaceville avengers.

'Well, McKay,' Morgan grinned without humour, 'we'll just start with you so's everyone here can see how wrong you are about that.'

The gunfighter lifted the engraved .44 in his left hand to level the weapon at Wheeler's chest. The pistol in his right remained positioned so as to cover the small group of Carlos, Juanita, and Abe. As Morgan thumbed back the hammer, his attention was focused upon Wheeler for an essential moment.

'Goodbye, McKay,' the gunman's eyes gleamed in expectation and the pink tip of his tongue slipped out to moisten dry, cracked lips. 'It ain't been nice knowin' you.'

Boom! Boom!

A Colt .45 sounded in the room, lead slugs punched two ragged holes in the shallow chest of Marshal Morgan Erskin. The impact of the bullets slammed his body against the wall, while a confused expression animated the man's pale features. His hands loosely held the big, beautiful revolvers as his eyes glazed and puzzlement turned to pain. A stream of scarlet leaked from his open mouth. The pistols fell to the sawdust to be joined by the crumbling form of the frail shootist sliding down the wall. In that brief, essential moment, Morgan Erskin had become a lifeless heap upon the floor of the big Grandview saloon.

'It took you long enough,' Wheeler grinned at the figure stretched out in the sawdust on the barroom floor. 'I was beginning to think you were gonna sleep through the whole thing.'

'Just wanted to give you a chance to handle everything on your own, son,' Chester Alison managed a feeble smile of his own. The deputy held his short-barrelled Colt .45 tightly in his right fist. 'Looks like old Morgan sorta forgot all about me.'

'His mistake.' Wheeler stooped to retrieve his Bowie, then located the Peacemaker and shoved the weapon home in the holster upon his right hip.

'Well,' Alison added, 'it ain't one he's likely to make again.'

'I thought you were dead!' Abe found his voice to join the conversation with a wide grin and a chuckle punctuating his words.

'Naw,' Alison responded in a low tone, 'just playin' possum is all. I figgered if I laid still long enough, Morgan'd count me out of things. When he made his move to plug Wheeler, I knew I had 'im. Howsomever,' he added in a voice growing hoarse and weak, 'now that the fun's over I could use a little patchin' up. I got a couple too many holes that need pluggin'.'

Carlos and Juanita stood locked in a warm embrace. The gunplay had ended. Grandview had been freed from the tyranny of the Box H rancher and town mayor, Jake Hollister. Furthermore, after years apart, Carlos was reunited with his family. There was magic in these moments among the carnage in the Grandview saloon.

Abe crossed the floor to the prone figure of Chester Alison in an effort to tend to the man's wounds. The flow of blood had already slowed to no more than a slight leak and neither of the two slugs had hit a vital area or bone. Wheeler joined them immediately.

'He'll be up and around in no time,' Abe announced after a brief inspection of the damaged deputy. 'You'll be sore for a while, but good as new before long.'

'Thanks, Alison.' The Croly County lawman knelt beside the older gunman. 'We appreciate what you've done and so do the people of Grandview.'

'Sure,' the hard man replied with an old note of cynicism creeping into his weary voice.

'Thunderation!' Isaiah 'Bullwhip' Wallace let loose with another enthusiastic exclamation. 'It is a blessin' to have you home, son!'

Wheeler and Bullwhip sat upon three-legged pine stools in the crisp, cool, early morning air of a fall day in south east Texas. Steaming mugs of thick, black coffee gripped tightly in their fists, the two old companions

197

enjoyed their reunion.

A week had passed since the barroom battle in Grandview. After bringing an end to Big Jake Hollister's oppression of the small south west Texas town, Wheeler had taken a day to assist the local population, Mexican and American, in bringing some order to the future. In addition, he had wanted to make certain that Chester Alison would receive proper care after the small band of riders from Wallaceville had pulled out for home.

Indeed, Alison now ranked as a local hero in the community of Grandview, Texas. The Mexican population, along with the handful of local merchants that had not been under the thumb of the Box H rancher, all agreed that the former deputy should now assume the role of marshal. Alison had agreed to take on the job. The ageing gunman would be on his feet again in a few days. At last, he had found the steady work that he had come to Texas in search of in the first place. This would be a good, honest job, with a future for a good man who deserved the people's trust.

'It's good to be home, Bullwhip.' Wheeler sat with little Michelle snuggled into his lap. Father and daughter were content with the nearness of one another after almost two weeks apart.

Wheeler and Abe had arrived late in the afternoon the night before. Exhausted from their trip, the two men had wolfed down a big meal before heading straight to bed. Relaxed and refreshed now, the Croly County lawman enjoyed the hot mug of coffee with his father-in-law, while Rosa Wallace and Laura McKay prepared a big breakfast in the kitchen out back.

'You say old Carlos Mendoza come through this thing all right?' Bullwhip asked for the second time that morning.

'Yes,' Wheeler smiled as Michelle gently nestled her head into the area under his chin, 'I'd sure say that he did. The sly old fox saved my skin with that big shotgun of his, and he held up just fine along the trail.'

'I can sure tell you that Ben Dalton had a fit when he found that note that Carlos left for him.' Bullwhip chuckled at the recollection of the Circle D rancher's consternation over his missing friend and servant. 'Claimed he'd have the old scalawag skinned alive.'

'Well, he'll have some good help now that Juanita has come back to the Circle D with Carlos.' Wheeler tickled the toddler along her ribs, bringing a delighted giggle from his daughter. 'Both Ben and Carlos can use a little help around that big house, and I believe that Juanita is just the young lady to do the job.'

'You're right about that one, son.' The old man scratched at his bushy beard with calloused fingers before taking a quick sip of the steaming brew. 'I sure got to admit we was surprised to see Abe Davis tag along after you as well. He followed after you as soon as you'd left for Wallaceville that mornin'.'

'No more surprised than me,' the young man confessed, 'but Abe is his own man. Like Carlos he took care of his end of the action and then some.'

'Speak of the devil…' Bullwhip began the old saying as Abraham Lincoln Davis crossed the ranch yard from the Bar W bunkhouse. 'Care for a cup of coffee, Abe?'

'No, thank you, Mr Wallace.' Abe stretched his big frame as he came to stand a few feet before Wheeler's seated form. 'It's good to be back.'

'Indeed it is, Abe,' Wheeler responded as he sipped a mouthful of hot, black coffee from the mug. Michelle hopped from his lap to toddle off inside the house in search of her mother. 'Thanks again for comin' along to Grandview.'

Abe merely shrugged his big, muscled shoulders. His deep brown eyes met Wheeler's. Obviously, there was something more to be said.

'Somethin' on your mind, Abe?' Bullwhip spoke up in his characteristically direct manner.

'Yes.' Abe shifted his attention to the grey bearded old man who owned the Bar W ranch. 'I'm goin' to have to be leavin' my job here around the end of the month.'

'What?' Bullwhip and Wheeler exploded in unison.

'Hold on!' Abe raised his hands for silence. His face broke into a grin. 'It looks like we're about to become neighbours.'

Confused expressions confronted the ranch hand, so he launched into a brief explanation. For many years now, Carlos Mendoza had held title to some two hundred acres of land along the small creek that separated the Bar W from the Circle D. Mendoza had never developed the property in any manner, since he devoted his years of service to his friend and employer, Ben Dalton. Now, Carlos planned to sell the property to Abe for the small bank account the giant had managed to accumulate over the past several years.

'Two hundred acres ain't much,' Abe concluded, 'but it's a good start for a small ranch.'

'That's a fine start!' Wheeler enthused.

'With neighbours like the Bar W and

Circle D,' Abe smiled from ear to ear, 'I just can't go wrong. I've found a place to settle down.'

'We're mighty happy for you, Abe,' Bullwhip interjected. 'In fact, we'll kick in a dozen head of cattle just to help get you off to a good start.'

'Thank you, Mr Wallace.'

'My friends and neighbours call me "Bullwhip".'

'All right,' Abe's handsome face beamed warmth and friendship, 'thanks, Bullwhip.'

'You say the word,' Wheeler added, 'we'll all be over to help you put up a house and barn soon as you're ready.'

'I'll be hollerin' for you, Wheeler,' Abe grinned. 'I've got to get out on the range. There's still work to do be done here on the Bar W.'

'Take it easy, Abe.' Wheeler waved to the departing cowboy. The giant simply wagged a big calloused hand in response as he crossed the yard to the corral.

'I suppose you stopped by Wallaceville on

your way in last night?' Bullwhip asked his companion before gulping down a big swallow of steaming liquid.

'Yeah,' the young man smiled again, 'I had to let Charlie and the gang know that the sheriff was back on duty. They fret like old hens when I'm away for a spell.'

Suddenly Laura appeared at the front door of the Wallace home with Michelle in her arms. The young woman seemed more beautiful than ever as a bright smile animated her features. There was no doubt that she was glad to see her husband home.

'You gentlemen about ready for breakfast?' She asked with a twinkle in her sharp, green eyes.

'I reckon so,' Bullwhip swallowed the remaining coffee from his mug as he stood to his feet.

'I'm sure enough hungry for a good home cooked breakfast!' Wheeler also stood as he held out his arms for the toddling daughter Laura had placed upon the hard packed earth that fronted the home.

'Papa!' Michelle called out as she ran into her father's waiting arms. Wheeler scooped the child up to hold her close to his chest.

'Tell Papa your new word, Michelle,' Laura prompted the toddler with a devilish look in her eye.

Wheeler turned a puzzled look toward his daughter, but Michelle only giggled before hiding her eyes against the young man's powerful shoulder.

'What's your new word, honey?' Wheeler asked of the squirming bundle in his arms.

Michelle met his gaze with a mischievous grin, then spoke the magic new word with clarity.

'Baby!'

Wheeler's confused expression turned to a wide grin as he shifted his gaze to Laura. His lovely wife nodded her head with a loving smile while she closed the gap that separated her from her husband. The three embraced for a warm family hug.

'Thunderation!' Bullwhip whooped his joy for the world to hear. 'Rosa, come a-runnin' and hear the news!' Rosa Wallace hurried out to be met with a strong hug from her happy husband. 'I'm gonna be a grandpappy again!'

The publishers hope that this book has given you enjoyable reading. Large Print Books are especially designed to be as easy to see and hold as possible. If you wish a complete list of our books please ask at your local library or write directly to:

Dales Large Print Books
Magna House, Long Preston,
Skipton, North Yorkshire.
BD23 4ND

This Large Print Book, for people
who cannot read normal print,
is published under the auspices of
THE ULVERSCROFT FOUNDATION